for Michelle

also by Roger Thyer-Jones

Dogs on the Runway

The Adventures

of Anna

Best wishes,

Roger.

Roger Thyer-Jones

Queen Anne's Fan

First published in 2022 by Queen Anne's Fan
PO Box 883 • Canterbury • Kent • CT1 3WJ

ISBN 9780 9573 639 7 7

A CIP record of this book can be obtained from the British
Library.

Set in New Clarendon 11pt on 13.4pt.

Cover illustration by Joe Wilson

www.queenannesfan.com

Printed in England.

Chapter One

No one noticed Burt as he leaned his huge bulk on the side of the van. Annoying snowflakes gently settled on to his bald head dripping into his eyes. Burt had watched Anna's homecoming with increasing anger. Christmas. He hated Christmas as much as he hated Anna.

He watched Anna sitting some thirty metres away surrounded by happiness and joy. He snorted. That dog was as good as dead.

No one saw him rest the self loading eighteen round rifle on the roof of the van, slowly releasing the cross bolt safety catch as he settled his arms and lowered his head into a shooting position.

He waited. He was motionless. He was waiting for Anna to turn her head towards him. He knew that it would happen. He would shoot the dog between the eyes. No mistake. It would be revenge. She deserved it. Also it would be justice for the way he had been treated.

The rifle trigger had to travel a long way. He pulled it slowly, feeling the cold metal under his finger. He knew that Anna would sense him and turn. He saw her head twist around and look directly at him. He saw her eyes widen with fear and recognition and smiled at the beginnings of her snarl.

This was his one and only chance and he was ready. He breathed out slowly and let the rifle sight settle on its target. He increased the pressure on the trigger just as their eyes locked together. He took the shot.

The bullet left the barrel travelling at over seven hundred metres per second. Nothing could stop it from killing Anna. Nothing.

May stood by the side of the grave with Lizzie, her eleven year old daughter. May was a slightly built woman with high cheekbones, almond grey eyes and auburn hair which made soft curls around her face. Her nose was small and straight. She was very attractive and in some light, almost looked oriental with her petite features. She had a small scar at the bottom of her chin as a result from falling over as a child and a gentle personality, but there was a vulnerability about her and a sadness despite all her efforts to be happy for her children.

She thought about her children.as she took Lizzie's hand. Lizzie was the eldest of three. She was of average height with a slim build, dark brown straight hair that fell to her shoulders and a wide, round face with a pointed chin. She had fair skin with a few freckles on her nose. Her eyes were big and blue and her nose was short and a little turned up at the end in a cute way. Lizzie was an avid reader and always looked serious but she had the loveliest laugh. She was thoughtful and very bright although May felt that she concealed this at school as she didn't want to be singled out by the others as a brainbox.

'Why did Dad have to die so young?' Lizzie asked, suddenly interrupting May's thoughts.

May looked at the two angels placed on the side of Jack's headstone but she barely saw them. She looked at the words of loss carved into the stone but those words were distorted by the tears in her eyes. It was still hard to believe that the love of her life, Jack, her American husband and the father of her children was dead.

'He had an accident, darling. Things can be dangerous in the Navy. You were only six, Eve was four and Alfie was just coming to two.

'What happened Mum? You never speak about it.'

'They said he fell through a trapdoor in his office which somebody had forgotten to shut.'

'What was a trapdoor doing in his office?'

'It was needed to get to the wiring and an electrician was supposed to be fixing something.'

'You sound as if you don't believe that it was an accident.'

'The letter they sent me said that an investigation had been carried out and his death was "misadventure". There was nothing more I could do. You've no idea how hard it was for me.'

'I didn't mean to upset you, I just wanted to know.'

May choked back her tears. 'You were all so young and didn't really understand but I had to be brave for you.'

'All I can remember is seeing the coffin with an American flag on it, being loaded onto the plane,' said Lizzie. 'I remember thunder and lighting in the sky and being sick over my doll, as the plane was tossed all over the place and sometimes dropped like a stone'.

May vividly recalled the agonies of having to accompany the coffin, together with her children, on the return flight to the UK. She had never felt so abandoned and alone. The spark had gone out of her life. Her eyes welled up with more tears as she relived the past joy of being with Jack. Her heart felt their intense love for each other and the deep chasm of sadness that she had fallen into when she lost him.

'Look darling, I knew that we had to stick together as a family with your Dad gone and I love you all so much. It was heartbreaking to see you trying to understand what had happened to our life.'

'Is that why you got us Anna? To help us get over Dad's death?'

'Yes. I never had a dog when I was growing up and felt that we all needed a fresh start to life. I decided that having our own dog to walk, play with and care for would cheer us all up.'

'I remember seeing Anna for the first time at that street market in London', said Lizzie, brightening up. 'She was just adorable. We all believed that she was a boy.'

'Yes and we first named Anna, "Sandy" because the man who sold us the puppy convinced us that Anna was male. How stupid I felt when Mr Ross, our neighbour, pointed out that in fact the dog was female. We all laughed so much.'

May thought about how Anna had grown over the years. She was a tall, fine looking bitch and her big chest and pointed ears gave off an air of confidence even though her right ear refused to stand up straight and flopped down on one side. She was a mixed breed, mostly German Shepherd, and had a lovely light brown colouration with some white patches on her chest. Her body was well proportioned, straight and strongly developed with muscular hindquarters and her outer coat had straight close lying hair that was quite dense but lovely to stroke. Her bushy tail hung in a slight curve

Anna's head was clean cut and fairly broad between the ears and her cheeks formed a softly rounded curve. Her muzzle was strong and her lips firm, clean and closed tightly. She had the most beautiful medium sized, almond shaped eyes which were dark brown. They seemed lively, intelligent and self assured. She was a lovely family dog.

'It was me that thought that she should be called Anna,' said Lizzie. 'I don't know why really, sometimes names just jump into your head. But why did you have to get rid of her? Why give her away to those awful men? I still don't understand it.'

May squeezed Lizzie's hand. Oh how they missed Anna. She had brought joy again to their family after so much sadness. May sighed as memories flooded back to her.

'Anna was a lovely dog and grew up playing with you children but never hurt any of you even when Eve tugged her fur and Alfie tried to sit on her back. We didn't really train her and the only command that we taught Anna was, "sit". But even without any real training Anna always seemed to know what we wanted her to do.'

'But you still haven't explained why, when she was so lovely, that she had to go. We all loved her so much and it broke our hearts.'

'You know she chased cats and she was too strong for me to hold. She would pull me over. I was the only one to take her out.'

'That's not fair. I took her out sometimes when my school work was done.'

'Anyway, she caught Mrs Jones's cat and nearly killed it. Mr Jones threatened me with the police if I didn't pay the vet's fee. I just couldn't cope with her anymore.'

You could have sent her away for training, or something. You didn't have to give her away,' said Lizzie angrily.

'Oh Lizzie, please try to understand. I was just trying to do my best for us all. I know that you were all hurt and I am so sorry that it happened.,

May thought about the events that led up to giving Anna away.

'You know Vicky, my friend?'

'The one that you sometimes go to the club with? I think that she never liked Anna'

'How can you say that? Vicky never said anything to me about not liking Anna. You need to be careful about saying things like that. Well, I told her about all the trouble I was having with Anna and she said that I ought to get rid of her before she killed somebody's cat.

'I told you that she never liked her. Anna wouldn't do that.'

'She very nearly killed Mrs Jones' cat and I just couldn't take a chance. There was a man in the club and he knew of a security company that would train her. He said that they had a good reputation and would take really good care of her.'

'You just believed him.'

'Well he seemed like a nice man and I didn't know what else to do. I was shocked when the next week, standing on our doorstep was the most enormous man that I had ever seen.'

'He was huge and his head was like a turnip.'

'His belly was bursting out of his trousers.'

'He had piggy eyes and a wobbly chin. I hated the way he looked at you. What was the name of the company he worked for?'

'I don't remember.'

'But you must have signed something for Anna. You wouldn't just hand her over.'

'It was all so sudden. I remembered signing some paperwork and passing Anna's lead to the man. She growled at him. It was obvious that she didn't like him and neither did I. I started to have second thoughts about letting Anna go but it was too late.

'Too late! How was it too late? You didn't have to hand her over.'

'Before I could change my mind, The man grabbed Anna's lead. Anna dug her paws into the ground in order to stop him from taking her and began to really growl and bark at him. I just couldn't bear to watch and went back into the kitchen, shutting the door.' May's eyes grew moist at the memory.' You must think that I am a terrible coward.'

'We watched it all happen from my bedroom window. We saw the man dragging Anna along the path towards the van. Anna was trying to look back at the house and we heard her whimpering. I opened the window and called out her name over and over again.

'That horrible man looked up at me and told me to shut up. Then another man, as thin as a pencil, came from behind the van with some sort of small harness in his hand. He put the harness over Anna's mouth and tied it tightly behind her head. She couldn't even bark.

'We watched Anna being thrown into some sort of a cage and heard the sound of the cage door clanging shut. I'll never forget that. The van doors slammed with a bang which made us jump. We were all crying and Eve and I hated you for giving Anna away. All we could think about was poor Anna alone and frightened, locked in the darkness of a cage and that we would never see her again. It makes me angry to think of it.'

'I know that you still blame me for giving Anna away darling. I tried to get her back. The next night I returned to the club and found the man I spoke to. I told him that I had made a mistake and asked if I could buy her from the security company. He said that he couldn't help and refused to talk to me any further. I am so sorry Lizzie. I just don't know how to make it up to you.'

May let go of Lizzie's hand and carefully placed the yellow roses that she had bought for Jack's grave into the aluminium pot that stood in the middle of the small diamond shaped green stones. She arranged the flowers in a pattern that was pleasing to her. Suddenly she pricked her thumb on a thorn and a drop of her blood fell onto the grave. May thought that Jack might still be with her if only he hadn't fallen down that trapdoor. She wanted Jack back but she strongly believed that he was waiting for her somewhere and some place in the future.

May didn't know if there was a God and sometimes thought that any God that could take her beloved Jack away was cruel and heartless. At other times she thought that perhaps there was a purpose to her life which she just couldn't understand, but that her children were precious to her and she needed to keep them safe.

'We could still look for her even now,' said Lizzie.

'Oh Lizzie, please don't keep on. I just don't know where she is or who she is with. I want her back but we just have to get on with our life,'

'You won't even try then.' Lizzie turned away from her.

May's fingernails bit into the palm of her hand as she clenched her fist tightly. She knew that she had made a terrible mistake but what had happened to Anna? Was there any way of getting her back?

Chapter Two

After a while, the van stopped. There was a bitter smell of smoke in the air. Anna tried hard to swallow but her tongue felt thick in her mouth and hurt her. She felt miserable, lonely and frightened. She heard doors banging and the sound of laughter.

At first she thought that laughter must be a good sign and relaxed a bit but the door of the van suddenly clanged open. The burst of light hurt her eyes. She could see two men. One was the man who had come to the door to take her away.

She tried to growl but the muzzle stopped her from opening her mouth. Burt bent down and easily picked her up.

'No use struggling and you try to bite me and you will regret it'.

'Easy on her Burt. She's just scared,' protested Joe.

'What do you know about training dogs, you idiot? Mind your own business or maybe I'll pick you up.'

'C'mon Burt, no need for that. I'm just trying to make sure that she's not injured or Mr Murphy will be angry.'

Anna felt helpless as she struggled in his huge arms, desperately trying to get down. She smelled water and all the hundreds of smells connected with a river. Then she heard furious barking. The barks of the males were long and threatening while the bitch's barks were of a lower pitch and slower, warning of danger.

Suddenly Burt threw her on to the floor of a cage in the yard. She felt a knee pressing painfully on her ribs and rough hands fumbled with the muzzle strap around her neck releasing it. Before she could take a bite at those hands, the door to the cage banged shut.

'Don't give her any food or water Joe until I say so. She needs to learn who is boss around here.'

In the next cage was a bitch. Her black eyes were piercing and she looked dangerous but Anna sensed her fear. She was whimpering which also made Anna feel very nervous. It was getting dark. Lights swept across the buildings and were so intense that she could hardly look at them. Dogs close by in other cages began to bark which set off other dogs in the distance barking too. Every bark seemed to be a warning of some sort.

Anna saw old buildings dotted around the yard. Some of them were falling to bits and looked abandoned. The yard had a bad atmosphere. Clear memories of the children in her home sustained her. She remembered the soapy smell of Lizzie, the sweet smell of Eve and the woody scent of Alfie. Those memories gave her some comfort in that hard, cold and unhappy place.

The security company, owned by Mr Murphy, used guard dogs to protect offices, warehouses and other places storing black-market goods. Burt was responsible for training the dogs, assisted by Joe.

Joe was never seen without a cigarette dangling from his thin lips. His hair was grey and straggly, hanging down to his shoulders in tangles. His eyes were close together and his nose was pointed. He had slender well kept hands with long fingers which were at odds with the rest of him. His frame was wiry and an old overcoat, dirty and torn in places, covered his stained security uniform. He seldom smiled and his face told a story of a hard miserable life.

'Get Anna out of the cage Joe. Give her some water but no food.'

'She has to eat Burt or she won't have no energy. Just let her have some scraps.'

'She eats when I say so. Now get her out of the cage and be quick about it.'

'Alright, alright. Keep your hair on.'

Joe unlocked Anna's cage and gave her a bowl of water. He nervously looked over his shoulder and saw that Burt was looking the other way. He quickly put some scraps of food down and Anna gobbled them up. Attaching a lead to her chain he led her out of the cage and handed the lead to Burt.

'She's in no shape for training yet Burt. She needs feeding up. Let her have some food and she'll be fine. She seems like a bright dog to me.'

'When are you going to learn to keep your mouth shut? Give her to me.' Burt pulled Anna's lead roughly towards him and she followed him. He stopped. 'Now. Sit'.

Anna used to sit down when May told her to, and so she sat and looked up at Burt. She expected to be patted on the head for obeying the command but instead Burt suddenly snapped a muzzle over her mouth. She hated that muzzle. She growled at Burt.

'Growl at me would you. I'll teach you to growl at me.'

Burt grabbed her head and put his hand on to her hind quarters thrusting her down to the ground. He took the chain from Anna's neck. He replaced it with something black and secured it.

'Don't use that shock collar on her Burt. She's just too weak and Mr Murphy won't be pleased if she's useless to him. That collar can give dogs heart attacks.'

'What? Do you think I'm stupid? I'll use the low setting just to liven her up a bit.' Burt laughed.' Just watch.'

Anna stood up and looked around. She could see that she was in a big shed. It was dark at the back of the shed and smelled of dead things. She wanted to get out and turned around in order to head for the open door but Burt pulled her back and told her to 'sit'again. She decided to try to make a break for the open door.

Suddenly red hot needles went through her neck and every part of her body shuddered. Her back legs gave way and she yelped as she fell to the ground, shivering uncontrollably and feeling very frightened.

Burt controlled the electrical current that would pass into Anna's body hurting her.

'Where do you think you're going? When I say, "sit," you had better sit fast or you will get a touch of the box.'

But Anna learned fast and knew what she had to do. Even though her legs were still shaky she sat down as fast as she could and whimpered to show that she meant no harm.

'That's enough for now Burt. You can see that she is shaky. Let me give her some food and she will be stronger tomorrow for training.'

'No food. I like them hungry. Put her back in the cage. I have to see the other dogs but I will really start her training tomorrow. She doesn't look like she will make the grade to me.'

'C'mon Burt, give her a chance. She needs to eat.'

'When I say no food, I mean no food,' snarled Burt. 'Get her back to the cage and shut up or maybe you'll be going in the cage with her.'

Joe led Anna back to the cage. He patted Anna on the head and shut the cage door.

'Don't you worry Anna; old Joe won't let Burt hurt you. Just be a good dog and do what you're told.'

Anna was alone in her cage and confused. How could her life change this fast? There was hardly any space in the cage for her to turn around. She had little water and no food. All the other cages were empty. She wondered where all the other dogs had gone. She looked up towards the sky and sniffed the air. She thought that it would rain soon for giant pillow clouds were heaping up in the sky, the air smelt peculiar and the wind was rising. The atmosphere felt oppressive. Something bad was coming. She had to get away. But how could she manage it without some sort of help?

'Where are you going Flo?' Sean asked in his soft Irish accent.

'Um, Just for a walk, Da, around the yard. Stretch my legs,'

'There's plenty to be done in the caravan. You haven't given it a good clean for a few days. Don't get lazy on me.'

Flo found that she was doing more and more to help out as she got older. She had to learn the right way of doing things and there were rituals to be followed. Washing up, for example, Cups would go first in the cleanest water because you put your mouth directly to a cup. Pots are always washed last, because the body has no direct contact with food from a pot; food goes from the pot to a dish. She would never eat directly from a pot, because they are not given the same special treatment as cups and are, therefore, not as clean. Sean was meticulous about cleanliness, as were all their family. Flo was also doing more of the cooking than she would have liked.

'You know I'm not lazy. Why are you always on my back? "Flo do this, Flo do that, clean this, wash that".'

'Don't give me any cheek girl. I've got enough on my plate at the moment without you starting up. I earn the money that keeps you and you have to pull your weight.'

Flo pulled on her old black lace-up boots, a brown top with faded writing on it and leggings. She threw the old black coat that was too big for her over her shoulders and grabbed a bottle of water. She put on her hair band with the white flower to hold back all her lovely red hair, which she hated. Her hair was scrunchy and inclined to hang down either side of her round face. No matter how she tried, her hair just wouldn't do what it was told and she had given up on it.

She had even features with brown freckles, but the most startling thing about her face was her enormous hazel eyes. She had a pretty nose and full lips, little ears and the loveliest smile which was infectious but she had a serious nature. Aged eleven, she was small but her posture made her seem taller and she was wiry and very strong. Her voice had a sing-song quality to it with a soft Irish accent, just like Sean's.

'What's upset you – besides being told to do your chores? Something is wrong'

'Um, I was thinking about Ma and how little I know about her. If she was here, I wouldn't have to do so much, You never talk about her. Why not?'

Flo sat on the bench seat inside the gaily coloured caravan where she had lived for years. Sean had looked after her for as long as she could remember.

'Leave the past alone. Too many bad memories.' Sean turned his head away from her.

'Please tell me about Ma and her family. I know that it hurts you to talk about her but I have to know. I need to know. I just seem to be different from the other girls and I just don't know why. What was she like? I'm not a baby; you have to tell me even if there are bad things.'

Sean shrugged his shoulders. 'Maybe it is time that you learnt about our past Flo, You're right. You are a bit different but I have always wanted you to fit in. It's been so difficult for me to raise you without your Ma being here, but I've tried my best. I've had to be hard on you with no Ma, so that you could look after yourself.'

'I know you have but I'm growing up now and you still treat me as a child,' said Flo, settling down and looking expectantly at him with her head turned to one side.

'I don't mean to. I'm trying to protect you. It's a hard world out there. But you deserve to know a bit more about our history.'

Sean sat down heavily and the caravan lurched to one side. His deep voice echoed in the caravan. 'Ah, now where to start Flo? Your Ma came from a proud background and was descended from Celtic singers, known as the Pavees. They were storytellers that lived in Ireland a long time ago. The Pavees used to make their living by moving from place to place telling stories and singing about life and love as well as battles, heroes and villains. Your Ma's family had a history of being great healers as well as being close to animals.'

'What do you mean, "close"?'

'Well, like they could speak to the animals and understand what they were saying. Sounds mad don't it?' Flo didn't reply but became very thoughtful. Sean continued, 'the Pavees were clever horse traders and were recognised as experts, respected for their skills and knowledge. Over the years the trade in horses and breeding horses came to a halt. They had to find other ways of making a living. Many outsiders said that the Pavees were thieves and troublemakers who ignored the law but this wasn't true although a bit of thieving went on.'

'We've always been outsiders. I have never felt like we belonged with normal people.'

'What's normal Flo? The Pavees made a living in a hard world the best way they could. As soon as a man made a profit, because he spotted an opportunity or simply outwitted an outsider, he was called a cheat or a thief. Pavees were often persecuted by the law and even when they tried to encourage outsiders to understand their way of life, they were driven away by hatred and prejudice. I am descended from them, your Ma was and so are you Flo.

'The Pavees had to stand up for themselves and always support each other. Outsiders called them travellers, gypsies or worse and they were used to being made to move on whenever they tried to stay for too long in one place. Often the Pavees had no choice to move when there was little welcome for them. Hatred was the reason why you couldn't go to the same school for long and had to learn from books at home. I know that you were often picked on at school, just because you lived a different life from other children of your age. That's why I had to toughen you up.'

'Yes. I'm a fighter. When I went to school,which wasn't that often 'cos you wanted me at home to do chores, it was always the same. I was picked on because the others thought I was different. You told me this would happen. They made fun of my red hair and my freckles. Being bullied, almost always ended in fighting. But I didn't want to fight, honestly, but when it happened I would just see a red mist.'

'Mmm, a chip of the old block.'

'I would attack. I didn't know any other way of fighting and I was fighting boys in our community since I was a wee girl. At school it always ended the same way. Someone would pull me off whoever was bullying me and had started the fight in the first place. I would then get the blame for being the bully. It just wasn't fair.

'Life isn't fair. It's the school of hard knocks that teaches you how to survive.'

'Are you listening or what? I so wanted to fit in and be kind and gentle and I never forgot it if someone was kind to me. When the bullying started I would try to walk away but then the bullying would always get worse. Half of the time I couldn't even remember what had happened in the fight but I never lost a fight, even with the bigger boys. Once I started then I would do anything to win. All I really wanted to do was learn and be like the other girls. I loved art and always enjoyed drawing and painting. I used to find my work ripped up or scrawled over when I went to get it the next day. The teachers didn't care. You've no idea what its like. I'm never going back to school.' Sean was a gentle giant. He stood well over two metres and weighed more than a hundred and sixty kilograms. He looked fierce and had the neck of a bull and a bashed nose. His ears were like cauliflowers having been battered almost daily since he was a boy. Tears came into to his eyes as he listened to her. 'I know that you were a fighting man Da, but were you picked on when you were young because you were so big?'

'That's a fine question and one that people seldom ask me. I was always big for my age and people thought that I was at least four or five years older than I was. They thought that I was simple minded as they had expected me to act older. I was called names like, "stupid ox," so I would fight and often get battered by the older boys until my Da taught me how to box. Once I knew that I had a hard punch then I could fight anyone and bullies left me alone, but I couldn't make friends easily. That's why I taught you boxing Flo.'

'You said that I had a hard punch too,' exclaimed Flo. 'But why did you fight so much when you were older?'

'I fought to make us money. In those days we fought in a ring made of bales of hay. No gloves were worn but there was a code between fighters. If you went down and stayed down then the fight was over. If you got back up to your feet, then you fought until the teeth were knocked out from your head. People bet big money on who would win and there was prize money to be had for the victor. I won a lot of money sometimes. They called me, 'Sean the Fist'.'

'You got hurt bad loads of times. I know, I saw your face after a fight. It was all bruised up.'

'Well, I'm not a fighting man now as I have a bit of a reputation and the challenges are few. I'm just a big old softy.'

Flo laughed and threw her arms around him.

'Why are we here in this dirty old yard? Even the name of the place is dirty, 'Mudchute'. How long do we have to stay? I don't like it here and I saw a man mistreating a dog in the yard. It upset me to watch him.'

'Don't worry Flo, no harm will come to you. I had some business with the boss who is distantly related to the Pavees that I told you about. This is an awful place. They train dogs for security work here and aren't very kind either. There might be more work from the boss for me before we go so we have to stay on for a day or two.'

Flo thought about the dog that she had seen being mistreated. She wondered again if there was a way to help the dog. She could normally get her way with Sean and twist him around her finger, but could she get him to do what she wanted this time?

She had noticed Anna as soon as they had entered the yard and parked up. Her name was on the cage. She saw her being cruelly trained by an enormous man. Flo hated cruelty of any kind and always sided with the victim. Immediately she wanted to help her.

She knew that she was different to other girls of her age and sometimes it really worried her. When she was with animals, such as dogs, cats or horses, she seemed to actually be able to speak to them. She could either say the words out loud or just think them. She didn't want to talk about her ability as she thought that other people would think that she was mad. But she knew just how bad Anna felt and sensed that unless she helped her, she might die.

Chapter Three

Early the next morning, Flo opened the door of the caravan and went to the cage where Anna lay. It was a bright morning and the rain had stopped during the night. But Anna was still miserable. She was thirsty and there wasn't even much rainwater to drink in her bowl.

Anna was very hungry and there was no food for her either. Her coat was already dull and matted with dirt from the shed floor. She looked exhausted. All the cages next to her were empty. Flo softly spoke her name, and Anna immediately opened her eyes and looked directly at her. She tried to stand up and Flo put her hand down to the bottom of the cage and gave her some of the small pieces of biscuit that she had found in her coat pocket. Anna sniffed the biscuits and then began to eat them. Those biscuits were only the second morsels of food that she had eaten for days and she gobbled them down. Flo found some more and fed them to her.

She heard voices coming from the shed and knew that she had to leave Anna and get away from her cage.

'Anna, I know that you can understand me. My name is Flo and I will help you but I have to go away now. Be strong, I will come back.'

Just as Flo was moving away from the cage she heard loud angry barks and men shouting.

'Shut those dogs up and get them in their cages. Tell old Joe to feed them. I'm going home,' said one of the security men.

Flo had to get back to the caravan, even though she

didn't want to leave Anna without food. If Sean came back and saw that she was gone, he would worry but she just couldn't get Anna off her mind and managed to sneak out again later and give her some more food without being spotted.

Anna was held near the river Thames in south London, in an awful place called Mudchute, near the Isle of Dogs. The yard smelt bad and there was a pungent smell of fish in the air as well. All the dogs were badly looked after and poorly treated.

Things got worse for poor Anna. Flo looked out of her caravan after she had had her breakfast and saw Burt standing in front of Anna's cage. She wanted to scream at him when he reached down to open her cage, grabbing her roughly by the chain and dragging her out. He put the black collar on her again. He held the black box in his hand and Anna trembled. Flo could see that he was talking to her and thought that he was trying to train her as she heard him say, 'sit' and saw that Anna had quickly obeyed the command. She was a fast learner.

Burt then pulled her up as he walked slowly forward. Every few steps he stopped walking and commanded her to sit. Anna looked confused and Burt pressed the button on the box again. A sharp pain filled Flo's head and involuntarily she flung up both arms to clasp her temples.

'Do what you're told and you won't get the box. What a useless dog.'

Flo just couldn't stand to watch Anna being hurt anymore and opened the door of the caravan running across the yard towards Burt.

'Leave her alone, leave her alone,' she shouted, clenching her fists.

'Well what have we got here? A little girl telling me what to do. Now ain't that a laugh? Just what do you think you are going to do about it?' Burt smirked.

'Leave her alone Burt,' said Joe appearing from the shed. 'Sean is her Dad and he's doing work for the boss,'

'Sean? I'm not scared of that old man. That gypsy scum shouldn't even be allowed to park that old piece of junk on our land and the boss will get rid of him soon anyway.'

'We're not gypsy scum. Just stay away from that dog.'

'Or else what?' Burt hitched up his trousers and took a step towards Flo, glaring down at her.

'Leave her alone Burt,' said Joe his voice trembling with fear.

Burt turned quickly and grabbed Joe by his coat shaking him like a rag doll. He flung him aside and Joe stumbled backwards holding his hand up to shield his face, fearing the blow that was coming.

Flo ran back to the caravan. She didn't really want to tell Sean what had just happened because she thought that it might cause trouble.

'What's wrong Flo? You look scared. What happened just now?'

Flo bit her lip. Failing to keep silent she said, 'I told Burt to stop hurting Anna and he threatened me. If it hadn't been for his mate, I think that he would have hit me. I know that you think that I'm mad, but Anna is in my head asking for help. It's weird, but when he turned on the box to hurt Anna, I felt it too. We just can't leave her here. Can't you do something?' Tears sprang into Flo's eyes and she turned her head away with embarrassment.

'Look Flo, I'll take care of Burt, but I told you that he doesn't own the dog. She's a fine looking bitch, not a thoroughbred, but she could have good looking pups if mated with a proper Alsatian. I know a man in Ireland who could help us and we could make money on the pups.

'This is the problem. Pat Murphy is the boss. Mr Murphy owns many businesses, some legal and some illegal but he also owns Anna. He is a hard man to deal with but he owes me a favour as I helped move some of his money about. You don't need to know the details. He just might sell me the dog. I'll talk to him this evening. If he agrees then we will take Anna with us. If not, then that is the end of it. Mr Murphy is a dangerous man and not to be messed about with, Flo. He would even try to hurt me if I crossed him so promise me that you will just deal with it and move on if his answer is "no".'

'If he won't sell the dog then what more can we do?'

'Good girl. I'll speak to him then.'

Flo loved Sean and would always obey him but somewhere inside her head she could hear Anna in her cage whimpering softly to herself alone and afraid. Or was she just imagining that she heard her? At that time Flo just couldn't be absolutely sure and it was driving her crazy. Every waking moment Flo was thinking about Anna and she knew that even if Mr Murphy refused to sell her, that would not be the end of it; promise or no promise. But why did Burt seem to hate her?

Burt hated everything about Anna. He thought that she had no spirit. He saw her as weak and cowardly lying there whimpering. He knew that she wasn't going to make it anyway as a guard dog.

'Why don't you like Anna, Burt?' asked Joe once in a burst of bravery.

'None of your business but as you ask, I was bitten by a dog just like her when I was a kid. The dog was chained up near our house and me and a mate were poking it with a stick. Just for a laugh really. We thought that the chain would stop the dog from getting near us but it lunged at me dragging its kennel a few feet forward. Bit my fingers and would have had my arm if I hadn't thrown myself backwards. Still got the scars after they sewed me up in hospital. Couldn't use my hand properly for weeks afterwards.'

'What did your Dad say?'

'I told him that we were just walking past the kennel when the dog ran out and bit me and that the dog should be put down. My Dad had a right go at the owner and got money out of him as compensation. Now you know.'

Sean was shaving and happened to look out of the caravan window and saw Burt mistreating Anna again. He remembered that Flo seemed to experience pain too whenever she was near her. He flung open the caravan door. Enough!

'Leave that dog alone. I'm going to buy her off Mr Murphy so don't touch her.'

Burt straightened his body and his fleshy jowls wobbled in fury as he turned his face towards Sean.

'Nobody tells me what to do with my dogs. Not gypsy scum like you.' He then walked towards Sean clenching fists which were bigger than Flo's head. His enormous belly quivered underneath his stained leather belt which was just about keeping his dirty trousers up. 'Well let's see what an old man like you can do then,' he grinned.

Burt made a bad mistake. He saw Sean take a step backwards and thought that Sean was afraid of him. But he had moved many times previously like this in fights and as Burt stepped forward, Sean's right hand crashed onto his jaw. Sean's hands were like hammers and if he hit a man, he stayed down. Burt's descent was almost in slow motion and his stomach threw up dust and dirt as he bounced and lay face down in a muddy puddle.

Joe came running out of the shed when he heard the shouting and saw Burt lying on the ground.

'You'll be for it now if you've killed him.'

'I just put him to sleep for a while as he was disrespectful to me. Throw a bucket of water over him to wake him up. He needs a wash anyway. You make sure that nobody touches Anna until I've done my business with Mr Murphy, or you'll get the same thing.'

Sean turned around and walked towards the old rusty steps that led up to Mr Murphy's dingy office. Now was the time to speak to him.

Flo had watched the fight from the caravan and was scared. The rain started to pelt down. The sound of thunder crashed nearby and lightning lit up the sky in ragged bursts of blinding light.

Some minutes later the door to Flo's caravan nearly came off of its hinges when Sean opened it and walked back in. His face was bright red and his fists were clenched almost as hard as his teeth. He was angry. Very very angry. In fact Flo had never seen him so angry.

'What happened?'

Sean turned his head slowly towards her and his eyes softened as he did so. He suddenly looked very old and tired. He flopped down on the sofa and the caravan lurched. He looked at Flo for a long time. Flo thought that he would never speak but she held her tongue.

'I tried Flo,' he said finally, 'I really tried but Murphy was angry with me for laying out that lump of lard Burt and he wouldn't sell me the dog. I told him that you had set your mind on that dog and I would pay his price.

'He said that our caravan had better be off his land by tomorrow or he would set his dogs on us. Even worse, he refused to pay me in full for the job that I did for him. I said that I would fight him for the money but Murphy just laughed and said that those days had long gone. I called him a coward and stormed out of his office saying that I would never again lift a hand to help him. In fact, I slammed the door so hard that the glass panel broke in it. I am really sorry Flo, I did my best and we will have to leave first thing in the morning without the dog.'

Flo put her arm around his huge shoulder to give him a cuddle.

'Umm, look Da, you really did your best and I love you for it but it didn't work out. We just have to accept it and hope that Joe, Burt's mate, will see that Anna is OK. The sooner we get back to Ireland the better. I had a dream that everything would work out although it doesn't seem like that now. I know that sounds weird. Do you think that Burt will come after you?'

'No, he might hate me but he knows that I can do the same again if he tries to hurt you or me. Don't worry about Burt, he's no threat to us. Get some sleep. We have to be off early in the morning. I'm going to turn in myself. Don't be late now.' Sean gave her a cuddle and kissed her on the forehead. 'Close the windows even though they will steam up. It will be a stormy night. Aah Flo, we did our best.' Sean poured himself a large whisky, closed the door to his bedroom and soon could be heard snoring loudly.

The light over the small table where they ate their meals was dim, but Flo could still see well enough to write. She pulled out a sheet of lined paper from her tatty old leather case where she kept her pencils, ruler, and reading books. She sat on the little white swivel seat at the table and chewed the end of her pencil. She began to write:

Dearest Lovely Da,
I told you that I had a dream. What I didn't say is that the dream was about Anna. As soon as I saw Anna I knew her and she knew me. Don't ask me how. Some things just are. I think that you understand

*this. I can't tell you about all the dreams I've had, but
I know that I have to set Anna free. I love you for the
way you stood up to Burt and tried to buy me Anna but
somehow I already knew that Mr Murphy wouldn't let
her go. I have to set her free and if I set her free then
we must escape from here. We'll be fine. My dream
said so. Don't try and look for me. We'll find you again
soon in Holyhead. It's all in the dream. You have to
trust me. Wait for us there.*

*I saved up some money from all the jobs I did so
we'll be OK. You have to leave in the morning and
drive to Holyhead. Stay at the camp outside the town.
You know where. You mustn't stay here or try to look
for us. I know that it will be hard for you to believe me,
but you mustn't, mustn't, mustn't look for us.
Somehow it will all work out. It's all in the dream. The
old woman told me. She knows us. You and I spoke
about her. She showed me the way. I think that you've
seen her too in your dreams and she seems kind. I have
to go now. Burt forgot to lock Anna's cage after you
did for him so it will be open.*

*I love you Da and know that you love me. Don't
worry, go to our usual campsite and wait for us there.
Trust me. Please.*
Love, hugs and stuff,
Your Flo
xxxxxxxxxxx.

Flo re-read the letter and tears sprang into her eyes
even as she fought them. She knew that he would be
upset but she also knew that she had to take action.
But would Da really understand?

She remembered that day when they talked about
the old woman who kept appearing in her dream.

'Last night I dreamed of an old woman with a red
head scarf with silver stars on it'

'Did you now?'

'She was telling me there was something that I had to do.'

'What was that?'

'It was about a dog.'

'What did the old woman look like?'

'She was very old, had big hoops of gold in her ears, sparkling eyes and a kind face. That's all that I can remember. Has she been in your dreams?'

'They are just dreams Flo. They mean nothing. Forget about her and the dog. Just dreams.'

But those dreams had now become a reality. Flo believed that Da would trust her but he would be very angry. Apart from stealing Anna, she realised that she had no plan except to escape with the dog from the yard. She believed that she was doing the right thing but was still full of doubts. She had never been completely alone and away from Da before. She was in a strange place and didn't have any idea about how she was going to get to Holyhead, even if she got clear with Anna. What would happen to her if Burt caught her?

Despite all her worries, she was determined that Anna was not going to spend one more night in this awful place

Storm clouds flew across the sky concealing the bright moon. The downpour made driving dangerous and cars swerved to avoid large puddles. The rain pounded on their little caravan so hard that it seemed as if steel ball bearings were hitting the roof. Lightning lit up the interior, throwing shadows into the corners. The shadows looked like little imps. Dogs howled and the wind shrieked.

Flo packed her little rucksack. She stuffed the few clothes that she was taking with her in the bottom and put her diary and pencils into the pockets of the rucksack. She then took her old battered teddy, with only one ear, and placed him on top of the other items.

'We will be safe won't we Ted?' Ted looked at her but didn't reply.

She thought that she would also need food and went to the small fridge. She slowly opened the door, shielding the little light in case it might wake Sean, but she could hear him softly snoring.

She took a lump of cheddar cheese from the fridge, some crackers from the cupboard and an apple from the fruit bowl. She had already bought dog biscuits for Anna and emptied what she had into a dustbin bag which she packed on top of her things including Ted.

'Sorry Ted.'

She put on two thick woolly jumpers, her leggings, socks and her boots jamming her old bobble hat onto her head and tucking all her hair underneath. Putting her flower hair band carefully into her pocket, she slipped on her waterproof jacket which had often saved her from a soaking, She gave the interior of the caravan, her home, one last look. She really felt that she was stepping into danger.

The wind fought her as she slowly opened the door. It almost tore loose from her grip but she managed to step out into the dark night and close the door without banging the door loudly. The rain stung her eyes but was losing its fury. Lightning lit up the yard and again the thunder rolled.

She could spot Anna's cage through the rain and saw that she was lying down, soaked and trembling with cold. Flo looked around her. Nobody was in the yard. She saw that the other cages were still empty. Where were the dogs? It didn't matter.

The yard was slippery and large puddles were filling the holes in its surface. She walked slowly and careful-ly. The glow from a lamp in the road cast just enough light to pick out the cages. The really bright lights in the yard had not been put on as yet. She was afraid to use her little torch in case someone would see the light.

Anna slowly stood up in her cage as Flo approached and watched her.

She spoke softly. 'Anna. Please, please don't make any noise.'

Anna stood up in her cage and looked at Flo. She wagged her tail. She could smell Flo's scent even as the wind tried to whisk that scent away. Her presence made Anna feel alive.

She got up and kept very still, almost like a statue. She could hear Flo's heart beating fast as she held her breath but there was no further noise apart from the rain beating down relentlessly. Flo cautiously felt for the hinge that usually held the padlock for the cage. The padlock was in place but was not locked. She slowly swung the arm of the lock sideways and freed the lock. The movement made a screeching noise. It was loud.

Flo stopped breathing and listened. A peal of thunder suddenly crashed in the air and she jumped but as she landed her boots splashed in the puddle and her hand rattled the cage door.

She heard a voice call from the inside of the shed. 'Anyone there? '

The shed door creaked open, spilling light onto the yard. Anna decided to bark. She tensed her mouth, her ears pricked up, her lips pushed forward exposing her teeth and she used her warning bark. Flo didn't know what to do but she let go of the cage, ducked down and hid by the side of it.

'Shut that bloody dog up Joe,' Burt said in a threatening voice.

'Alright, alright,' Joe replied. ' Shut up Anna!'

Anna stopped barking. The wind blew fiercely and the rain continued to lash down. Joe closed the shed door and the light disappeared. It was dark again in the yard and the main lights were off. Anna turned her head to see Flo still crouching by the side of the cage. She licked her lips and cocked her head trying to encourage her to hurry.

Flo understood her urgency for freedom and came up from her crouch. She quickly moved around to the front of the cage. This time she fully opened the door. Anna still had the black collar around her neck as well as the chain and Flo bent over trying to find the clasp in order to undo it. Her fingers trembled. The clip was stiff and Anna stood as still as she could until finally the clasp came undone and she was free from collar's menace.

Flo thought that she had whispered to Anna, telling her to stay close and to keep quiet. It was strange, but once again she could not be sure if the words were in her mind or if she had actually spoken them.

The wind picked up leaves and pieces of scrap paper blowing them across the yard as the rain hit their faces, stinging their eyes. Anna padded silently across the yard following Flo towards the black iron gate at the back of the shed that led on to the street.

Flo had been through that gate many times to go to the local shops returning with food for her and Sean. She knew that Burt didn't keep it locked during the day but what about if he locked it at night? They would be trapped.

They crept up to the gate. She pulled the metal handle but the gate didn't budge. Panic set in. Her heart beat faster and faster. Anna licked her hand, trying to calm her. The gate was locked. Flo calmed her breathing and her heart beat slowed. She stretched her hand up to the top of the gate towards the bolt.

She pulled back the bolt slowly. But the bolt was stuck. Her little arms couldn't pull the bolt hard enough to free it as it was above her head. She looked around for something to stand on and saw an old oil drum nearby. Slowly and carefully she rolled it over towards the gate trying hard not to make a sound, but the wind was still howling and covered any noise that she made.

She climbed on to the oil drum, very nearly falling off as it swayed dangerously under her weight. Anna put her side against the drum and tried to help with the balance. With the extra height, Flo could reach the bolt with both hands. She pulled the bolt. The bolt slid and stopped. She pulled again and this time the bolt moved right out of its holder and slid across. Flo got down from the oil drum, which wobbled but didn't fall, and found her feet splashing into a puddle as she did so.

Now the gate must surely open. She pulled on the handle. Nothing happened. Anna sensed her panic. Once again she licked Flo's hand and Flo controlled her breathing and calmed down. Anna pawed the bottom of the gate and Flo bent down to see what she was doing. Another bolt prevented the gate from opening. She pulled. The bolt slid back easily. At last she could open the gate. She gave the handle a pull but as she did so her boots slipped in the mud and she fell backwards.

Unfortunately she fell straight against the oil drum. With a crash the drum fell onto its side. The drum then rolled slowly away towards the shed. Flo flung up her hands to her face in horror. Bang. The drum hit the shed making a loud hollow noise. It bent the drain pipe holding up the gutter. The gutter fell to the ground with a crash spilling rainwater and smashing into the side of the shed window.

The shed door was flung open as Burt and Joe ran outside.

'What the hell is going on,' Burt roared, 'Where's that bleedin' dog? Her cage door is open. I can hardly see anything in this rain. Joe, run to the cage and see if she's escaped.'

Joe ran out into the yard dressed in just his t-shirt and jeans but with no boots on his feet. He had a torch in his hand and the rain stung his eyes, blinding him. It seemed like the elements were fighting him and trying to stop his progress.

'I can't see much in this rain but the cage is empty,' he yelled.

'Never mind the cage,' shouted Burt, tightening the belt on his trousers. 'Check that the gate is shut and do it now.'

Joe ran around to the back of the shed. His torch sent a crazy beam left and right as he stepped over the fallen gutter. His sodden feet slipped in the mud and he fell on his face into a puddle. The last thing he saw as he lifted his head and wiped away the mud from his eyes was Anna and Flo escaping.

Chapter Four

It was night but the glow from the few street lamps helped Flo to see. They had left chaos behind them. Flo could hear the sound of an engine starting up, the banging of doors and the angry shouts of men. It was dark and the rain lashed at her eyes as Anna ran beside her. Flo kept slipping as she ran across the wet pavement.

Flo turned her head left and right scanning the road ahead and looking for trouble. She was running away with Anna but where were they running to? She could still hear the loud sound of a rattly diesel engine. It was the same as the sound made by the van owned by Burt.

She knew that unless they moved quickly and kept to the shadows that Burt would find them both. Oh no, Flo suddenly heard the sound of dogs barking excitedly. Those dogs would be coming after Anna's scent and would track them down.

When Flo smelt fish she had a thought – fish masks smell. Sometimes the smell of fish in Mr Murphy's yard was so strong that it overpowered all other senses. This smell came from nearby. She thought that if they could get to the place where it was at its strongest then they could hide and at least the dogs would not be able to smell Anna. Flo was not exactly sure about this but at least it was a plan of sorts.

Anna brushed against her leg, startling her, but she kept on running. Anna brushed against her leg harder this time almost making her lose her step. Flo stopped.

'What is it Anna? We have to run. This is no time for playing games.'

Anna stared up at her Flo and concentrated her mind

on the smell of fish as hard as she could. Anna turned her head in the direction of the smell and wagged her tail. She walked a few paces and stopped once again turning her head to look at Flo. At last Flo understood what she wanted her to do.

'You want me to follow you Anna? You know something to help us? OK let's go.'

Anna ran in front of Flo just fast enough for her to keep up. They kept to the shadows and avoided the lights of the few cars that moved quickly up and down the road. Flo could hear the dogs barking and they were getting nearer but all the time the smell of fish was getting stronger then she suddenly realised that they were very close to Billingsgate Fish market

'Oh Anna, that's brilliant. You are following the smell. If we can hide there the dogs will never find us. I love you Anna.'

They ran over bridges and past boats moored on the wharves. It seemed like only a short time before they were approaching the market. There were bright lights and lorries entering and leaving the entrance to the market. Flo heard shouting, not the angry shouting that she had heard in the yard, but shouting that sounded happy and excited.

She saw men moving quickly in and out of the shadows in front of a huge hall that reeked with the overpowering smell of fish.

Suddenly she staggered and stopped. She rested against a wall, turning her head slowly. She felt confused. For an instant she had seen a vision of a boat that was gaily painted with flowers on the side. The boat also had a strange sign painted on its side with writing underneath. Strange. Very strange. What did the vision mean ?

She shook her head and refocused her eyes. Anna had stopped in front of her and was looking back. Flo pushed herself away from the wall and looked closely at the market entrance which was in front of them. She saw a lorry being loaded with containers full of fish. Flo looked at Anna uncertain about what to do.

'What now Anna? Do we hide among those empty boxes at the side of the building? We must do something as I can hear the dogs coming nearer.'

Flo knew that time was running out and that the tracker dogs would soon be on their heels. She watched the driver of the lorry standing in the pouring rain and talking to the man who was loading the fish. They shook hands and the driver turned towards the front of the lorry. The back of the lorry was still open and she knew that they could easily jump up onto the tailboard if only they could sneak past the guard on the gate. Flo looked about on the ground and saw an old beer bottle lying there. She picked it up. She took aim and threw it high in the air on the other side of the gate to the security hut. It smashed. The door to the hut quickly opened and the guard ran out to investigate what was happening. He crossed over the road by the gate. It was their chance.

They ran out of the shadows and around the security hut crouching down behind an old tree near the wall. The guard looked around him, kicked the broken pieces of the bottle onto the grass and then walked back into the hut, closing the door as he did so.

'Drunken idiots. They might have hurt someone.'

The tailgate of the lorry was close by. Flo looked at Anna and then looked at the tailgate. Anna seemed to understand what she needed to do.

There was no time to lose. They began to move slowly and carefully out of the shadows. The coast was clear and in several bounds Anna crossed over the road and jumped up onto the tailboard and into the back of the lorry with Flo following close behind. They moved to the back of the lorry treading on slippery smelly fish that had spilled out of the iced containers.

The smell was awful. Flo held her nose as she found her way to the corner where Anna sat. She sat down beside Anna putting her hands around her neck. Anna nuzzled her and licked her face.

The tailgate of the lorry crashed shut. They were in complete darkness until Flo put on the small torch light which shone on to the lorry's cargo of crabs, eels and fish. She could hear fish sloshing about in the plastic containers. Some more fish had spilled out between the containers when the catches had popped open and the torch light flashed on to their silver scales making Flo shudder. The dark interior of the lorry was frightening and her heart was beating fast. The air was thick and heavy with the smell of fish which made her head spin. But there seemed to be no air in the back of the lorry and Flo and Anna started to gasp for breath.

Anna could smell a current of cold air coming up between one of the wooden boards that lined the floor. She stood up and walked over to the small gap pawing it with her front paw until Flo followed and lowered her head to the hole.

'I can just get my finger into the hole and the wood is rotten. I think that I can open it up,' Flo whispered.

Flo pulled at the rotten plank which gave way in her hand and immediately she could see the road rushing past below. Fresh air, mixed with petrol fumes, poured into the lorry but at least they could both breathe. Flo sat down and put her head in her hands.

'Oh Anna, Anna, what a mess we are in. Where are we going? Did I do the right thing to escape with you? What about my Da? Oh Anna, what are we going to do now?' Tears sprang into Flo's eyes as her hands entwined the fur at Anna's neck but Anna seemed very calm and her calmness gave Flo confidence. She closed her eyes. A white mist swirled in her head and it felt as if someone was speaking to her in a strange language but the sound was soothing.. Someone who was old like a spirit but without any form. Flo wasn't frightened and sensed that they had done the right thing by jumping into the lorry.

When she opened her eyes she realised once again just how dangerous their predicament was. They were trapped inside a lorry which stank of fish and had no plan about what they were going to do next. She started to feel very anxious again.

Pat Murphy did not like being woken up in the middle of the night and being dragged into his office. He was in a foul temper. He had a blinding headache and he wiped his cold, damp forehead with the back of his wrist

In the dark office above the yard, Burt and Joe shifted nervously on their feet in front of Murphy's old oak desk.

Murphy thought about his past. He had grown up in the slums of Dublin. There was always trouble. With four brothers and three sisters there was never enough to eat in the house. His father was rarely at home and when he did come home he was usually drunk and abusive.

His mother did her best to raise the family on her meagre income which she earned from cleaning posh people's houses. It was no wonder that nearly all his siblings were involved in crime of some sort. Stealing was just a way to survive and in his world, you either survived or you went under. All he could recall of his childhood days was fighting – fighting at school when he attended, which wasn't often, fighting in the streets and later fighting in gangs.

He vividly remembered the day that he had been walking home after scrounging for scraps near the docks. He had unwittingly walked into the territory of a rival gang.

'What are you doing in our territory? You are

thieving here. Turn out your pockets. What's that around your neck ? Give it here.'

'No, take the money I have but leave the cross. Please leave the cross. My Grandma gave it to me.'

'Who cares about your old grandma? Give it here.'

He remembered running away as soon as he could get to his feet while they jeered, throwing rocks and stones after him. Every part of his body hurt from their blows and they had robbed him of the few pence that he had. Worse, they had taken his only treasured possession: the cross that his grandma had given him before she died.

He had never seen anything so beautiful and she told him to put it on, keep it well hidden and safe. When he left her, some hours later, his Mum had told him that she had passed away. He often sat alone in his bedroom, thinking of his Grandma, just holding the cross in his hand and watching the light bounce off the golden filigree which was woven into intricate patterns. He would examine the pearl at its centre admiring its smoothness and sheen. The pearl was always warm to his touch. That cross was the only thing that he had ever really possessed and he loved it. He had kept it well hidden, even from his family. When it was stolen from him, he felt as if a part of him was lost as well.

But he had clawed his way up the greasy pole of crime. In a brutal world he had excelled at brutality until he ran crime in nearly all the parts of the city that he controlled. He also had dingy bolt holes in nearly every city in the UK including Mudchute in London, where he had his yard.

Years ago, he had made a promise to himself. Nobody would ever take anything that was his again without the full force of his anger coming down upon them. He never forgot that cross and had hunted high and low for it but without success. He often touched his neck feeling for it even though he knew that it was gone forever.

He couldn't care less about Anna. Anna was nothing to him. But he had told Sean that he couldn't have the dog and that was that.

Now his dog, his property, was gone. Stealing from Pat Murphy was also bad for his reputation. His word was law in the jungle that he lived in. To break that law meant punishment and Pat Murphy could be merciless when it came to revenge.

Burt's huge jowls trembled and his belly wobbled as he stood in the uncomfortable silence. He knew enough not to speak unless Mr Murphy spoke to him. The silence was unnerving.

'Who left the cage open?'

Burt froze. 'It was Joe's responsibility to lock the cage.'

'You was the one who put her in the cage, not me!' Joe spluttered. 'Burt, you can't put the blame on me. Honest Mr Murphy I always lock cages.'

Murphy looked at them both with an evil glitter in his eyes.

'One of you, or both of you, will be meeting my dogs in the kennels if you don't bring that dog back, together with that girl and her dad.' His voice oozed with menace.

Both Burt and Joe gulped and Joe's nose began to run. Burt had trained those kennel dogs and he knew that they could rip a man to bits in seconds. Mr Murphy was not a man to make idle threats.

'You have until Christmas Eve to sort it out. It will be my Christmas present,' he paused. 'Either way.'

Burt and Joe looked down at the floor.

'You won't catch them staring at the floor you idiots, now get out.'

Burt and Joe scrambled for the door and clattered down the iron stairs glad to be out of the office.

'You left the cage door open Burt. Why blame me?'

'Shut up. If we don't get that dog back we'll both be for it. Now let's get to work. We have to find them. It can't be hard to find a girl with a big dog. Put the word out on the street that there is a reward for any information. They won't get far.'

Once his men had gone, Pat Murphy brought both his hands up to his temples and slowly massaged them hoping that the pain in his head would ease. Doctors? he thought dismissively. Useless. None of them seem to be able to cure this stabbing pain.

He reached for the whisky bottle that he kept in his drawer and took a deep slug. The whisky numbed the pain for a bit but then the pain viciously bit into his head. He knew that the pain wouldn't leave him. Another sleepless night in agony.

The lorry rattled along the road and the plastic containers of fish bumped against each other. Flo could hear eels slithering in a nearby container. She didn't like that sound. Flo held Anna's head gently stroking it and Anna could feel her trembling.

Time stood still but eventually Flo could feel that the lorry was slowing down. Flo sensed that they were very near their destination and slowly stood up, holding on to a wooden plank at the back of the lorry. She wobbled.

'Anna, I think that we are near a place where we can get out of this awful lorry.' She was breathing heavily and holding her nose.

Anna raised her front paw and put it on to Flo's little hand just as the lorry lurched to a halt. Flo fell over hitting the side of the lorry. The noise was quite loud. She heard the driver's door open and then slam shut. All was silent except for the sound of the slivering eels. Flo held her breath.

Flo heard the sound of voices talking in a friendly way outside the lorry. There seemed to be two men chatting. Suddenly the tailgate of the lorry opened with a crash.

Anna turned her head to look at Flo and started to walk slowly and carefully forward over the containers. Flo followed her as carefully as she could but it was still dark and she couldn't use her torch in case of the light being seen.

As Anna slowly stepped over the partially dislodged lid of one of the containers she brushed against something hard. A red hot pain shot through her paw. She gave a yelp.

Flo looked inside the container.

'It's a crab. A crab has pinched your paw. Hold still. I'll get it off.' She heard a voice outside the lorry.

'Did you hear that? It sounded like a bleedin' dog. Get a torch from the cab.'

Flo managed to get the crab to let go of Anna's paw and as they both moved towards the tailgate a torch shone straight into her eyes, blinding her.

'What the–?'

Just as the driver started to speak Anna leapt out of the tailgate closely followed by Flo who jumped down behind her. Still partially blinded, Flo landed in the road just as one of the men tried to grab her and she nearly slipped. As she straightened up, the driver grabbed her by her coat bringing her to an abrupt halt.

'Got yer. Stand still and don't move.'

The driver was watching Flo and so he didn't see Anna turn back and come towards him from underneath the lorry. Anna nipped him on the backside. The driver jumped up in the air, letting go of Flo's coat and as he landed, he slipped on the wet road and collided with the other man standing next to the lorry. They both fell over in a tangle of arms and legs.

Flo quickly jumped back onto the pavement and with Anna beside her they ran across the bridge. She spotted a dark alleyway and turned into it, breathing heavily. She heard the sound of the men coming after them. She sensed that she was near the place that they needed to be but, once again, was confused. She saw the glint of water under the bridge.

In a flash her dream came back to her. She recalled a canal. There was a narrow boat with flowers painted on the side. No, that wasn't right. There was a sort of shape with a circle and star in the middle of it and two banana shapes underneath the circle on either side. Anna's name was written below the shapes.

Flo ran forward and Anna followed her until she came to steps. Those steps led down to a lock. An old fashioned lock with heavy swing gates. There was a dark tunnel leading away from the lock. The lighting in the lock was dim, barely casting enough light to see clearly.

Suddenly the clouds parted briefly to reveal a full moon, the winter moon, shining brightly. It seemed to float above their heads. Flo stared and her mouth dropped open in surprise. The moon briefly lit up the lock before the clouds closed around it once more, leaving the lock in gloom but in that instant she had seen a narrow boat which sat low in the water. The boat was almost invisible in the tunnel outside the lock. Flo could make out painted flowers on the side. She also saw a shape. Her eyes were drawn to the shape as if she were hypnotised. All was quiet in the lock but she could hear the sound of traffic in the road and angry voices. Boots clattered across the bridge.

She felt trapped. It was now too dark to see the path that led along the canal and into the tunnel where the boat lay. They had to move and move quickly.

'Anna, quick, let's go. This is the boat I saw in my dreams but there seems to be no one on it. We will have to go down that path and hide in the bushes. Perhaps they won't find us.'

They began to move down the lock path and there was a smell of sweet smoke in the air wafting towards them. The smell was coming from the narrow boat.

Could there be someone inside? They were so close to the stern they could easily have jumped on to it but all was dark. Flo looked behind her and saw a shape. It moved as quick as lightning and seemed to flow across the gap between the path and the boat, grabbing Flo in one movement, sweeping her up and moving back the way it came. She didn't struggle.

Anna jumped and landed in a heap on the stern just as the shape holding Flo, who was now asleep, moved down the small stairs that led into the dimly lit interior of the boat. Anna jumped down those stairs and skidded to a halt bumping into a table.

The dark shape ran back to the door leading from the stairs and shut it firmly. Door locks closed. All was in darkness. Flo was now on a couch sleeping peacefully with the sweetest smile on her face. A blanket covered with silver moons was over her.

Anna also felt at home and at peace as if someone had wrapped her in love and was whispering words that she didn't understand but knew that they meant security.

Bang Bang Bang.

'Open the door.'

Band Bang Bang.

'Open the door or I'll smash it down.'

Bang Bang BANG.

All was quiet inside the narrow boat. No light showed.

'Come on, there's no-one there. They must have given us the slip in the road. You can't hide a girl and a big dog here. What a night. Who would believe it?'

'In my lorry, trampling on my fish. A girl and a dog. I'd better tell the police about it. I smell smoke. I bet someone's hiding in there.'

'No time for that. I need my fish unloaded. None of our business anyway. No harm done. Just some urchin and her dog getting a free ride. Come on mate, let's get out of here.'

Heavy boots clattered up the stairs and went back onto the bridge. Flo and Anna had escaped again but who or what had rescued them?

Sean read her note in disbelief. He knew that she was headstrong but to steal Anna away from Mr Murphy was just crazy. He knew that Burt wanted to hurt Anna badly or even kill her. Sean felt that he had tried his best to buy Anna from Mr Murphy. He shook his head. How could she have done such a stupid thing especially when he had told her that Pat Murphy was not a man to upset. Sean thought that Flo had accepted the situation and moved on.

Now he knew that he had a real problem. Murphy's men and dogs were gone from the yard chasing after Anna. If he stayed in the yard then Murphy would have him hauled in for questioning; he would just not believe that Flo had kept her escape route secret and had not spoken to Sean about it.

Then was there was nothing for it. He would have to leave the yard immediately and try to find Flo and Anna as he drove along the road. If he couldn't find them then he would drive to Holyhead and wait there. He banged the table with his fist. How on earth would Flo get to Holyhead without help? What if Murphy got hold of her? He would use her to get to Sean. There would be consequences. Sean didn't scare easily but he knew trouble when he saw it.

Murphy would be looking for his caravan and so he would have to get rid of it on the way and find different transport. Fortunately Sean's contacts, who were related to the Community, owed him a favour or two. He would arrange for new transport and then make his way to the meeting place. What else could he do ? He couldn't involve the police. No self respecting member of the Community ever went to the police. Problems were sorted out the old fashioned way.

The meeting place. Sean knew that Holyhead was known as the Holy Island and was separated from Anglesey in the West by a very narrow channel. Traffic crossed to the island over a causeway. The port of Holyhead was a busy ferry port where ships operated to and from Ireland. Holyhead has linked Ireland to the Holy Island for over four thousand years bringing boats and ships across the sea.

Even if he went to the campsite where they sometimes stayed on the Island, there remained the problem of not knowing when, or even if, Flo and Anna would arrive in Holyhead. Additionally, Murphy's men would be on high alert and a young girl with a big dog would be easy to spot. He banged his fist on the table again. Everywhere his mind went there was a problem and no easy way to solve it.

Every problem had a solution but now his problems seemed to be growing from hills into mountains. Still, he had to start somewhere and staying in this yard was just not an option. His heavy shoulders sagged with worry as he climbed into the seat of the old Land Rover that towed the caravan. He slumped heavily down onto the battered driver's seat, put the keys into the ignition and started the engine which spluttered into life. The Land Rover slowly took up the weight of the caravan and Sean eased forward towards the open yard gates anxiously looking around for trouble.

There was nobody in the yard as he drove out into the road with the wind rocking the caravan and the rain battering at his windscreen.

Sean didn't often talk to God but he did now.

'Please God keep them safe. 'Keep them safe.'

Chapter Five

Flo felt a movement. She heard the sound of water swishing, murmuring, and whispering. She lay as still as a tiny mouse fearing that a cat was waiting to pounce. She wasn't afraid but she did feel anxious. She could only remember running towards the boat, seeing Anna's name and then sinking into a deep sleep. She snuggled comfortably under the warm blanket.

Sunlight shone through the portholes of the boat giving the cabin a warm glow. The sweet smell of wood burning and incense drifted the air. The interior of the boat was exciting. Varnished wood gleamed in a honey colour and lined the cabin walls. There were bright paintings of summer scenes, gaily painted castles with flags fluttering from the battlements, and horses prancing in green fields.

Everywhere she looked there were patterns painted on cupboards, doors, even on the ceiling. The patterns were astonishing. They were complicated and interwoven, showing bright reds, greens and yellows so closely entwined that the lines seemed to be alive as they twisted and turned around each other.

Lace was everywhere. Lace hung across the tops of the curtains. The table next to her couch had a lace tablecloth on top which looked very old. There was a lace curtain hanging in front of an arch that led to the stern of the boat. Red and blue cushions with strange shapes woven into them were scattered across the cabin. The whole atmosphere felt magical, as if she had entered into another world. She wondered if she was dreaming.

Except for the water lapping against the side of the

boat, all was quiet. How long had she been asleep? She noticed that Anna was still peacefully sleeping curled up on the floor on a soft blanket.

'You're awake then?'

The voice had a beautiful sing-song Irish lilt to it. Flo turned her head and there stood an old woman. She wore a white blouse and a long red skirt which was woven into multicoloured strands and seemed to billow out from her. A headscarf, which was bright yellow and had tiny pictures of cats and dogs stitched into the fabric, covered her hair. A gold chain hung from her neck. The chain had exactly the same pattern that Flo had seen painted on to the side of the boat. The woman was small and plump. Her grey hair cascaded out from under her scarf but Flo was drawn to her eyes. They were green and sparkled as if touched by fairy dust. Her skin was brown and wrinkled, kissed by the sun and on her hand rings of every description and gemstones of red and green caught the light, sending diamond patterns on to the cabin walls.

'Come on Flo, sit up. You will have many questions for me but I think they can all wait until after breakfast.'

The old woman turned and disappeared behind the lace curtain and Flo could hear her singing softly to herself in a strange language, as well as the clinking of knives and other kitchen sounds. Soon she returned with hot mugs of tea, bread, ham, tomatoes, honey and jams. The table next to Flo filled up quickly. The old woman put a bowl of food on the cabin floor for Anna. There was fresh water for her too.

'Now eat Flo, and Shelta, for that is my name, will tell you why I had to save you and Anna. You're safe here with me for now so don't worry. Nothing bad will happen but I know that there are men hunting for you. Tell me your story. No hurry.' Shelta settled herself down on the comfortable chair opposite the couch and waited expectantly.

Flo's mouth was filled with the delicious bread and creamy cheese. She screwed up her eyes deciding where she would start her story. She was surprised to see that the mug of tea that she held in her hand, had a painting on the side of a dog just like Anna.

'I don't know where to start. It all happened so fast but I'll try to make sense of it.'

She started to speak slowly but her words became a torrent as they tumbled out of her mouth. She told Shelta about Burt and their escape from the yard, describing the trip in the fish lorry which made Shelta laugh. She shared her worries about Sean and the letter she had left him with a plan to meet up in Holyhead and escape to Ireland. She described her dream and spoke about the old lady who seemed to be guiding her.

Shelta nodded when she heard this.

'Sure I had a similar dream about one week ago and the old lady in it told me to take my boat to London near a canal that smelt of fish. Your name and Anna's name came to me. When I woke, I just could not get the dream out of my head and changed all my plans. The only canal that I could find that might smell of fish was near Billingsgate, the fish market and so I headed there, stopping on the way to pick up a few things that I thought might come in handy.'

'I saw Anna's name on the side of the boat. How could that be?'

'Do you know what a rune is?'

'No.'

'It is invisible to anyone other than the person that it is intended for and is there to protect the person, or animal, named in it. Your names were sent to me in a dream and so I painted the rune with Anna's name. That's why you and nobody else could see it.'

'I have to get to Hollyhead and find my Da. Then we

have to get to Ireland. Anna will be safe there as Da knows people that can protect her. We must find a way to make peace with Mr Murphy. It is all so difficult and I feel lost.'

Shelta was quiet for what seemed to be a long time.

'Our paths have crossed because they are meant to. The lady in your dreams was your Ma's Grandma. She was a famous healer and had the second sight. She had many talents and could talk to animals. But outsiders called her a witch and she met a sad ending. You don't need to know about it. She could see the future which was a blessing and a curse and was loved and respected in our community. Do you ever have dreams in which you are flying? Do you sometimes feel that you can speak to Anna without actually saying words?'

'How did you know that? I often get frightened by my dreams and fly to strange places. Sometimes I'm afraid that I won't be able to get back. Since I was young, I always seem to know what animals want or if they are happy or sad. When I'm with Anna, I often don't know if I am actually speaking to her or if it is all in my head. It's like speaking to a person using a tin can with a bit of string attached to another tine can. I can hear words but sometimes they are fuzzy but I seem to pick up the emotion in them. I know how Anna is feeling. Every now and then, when I am with someone who is in pain, I can feel that pain as well. It really scares me.'

'Do you ever put your hands on someone in pain or an animal who is hurt and lessen the pain for them?'

'Yes and that frightens me as well.'

Shelta sighed. 'We are going on a journey that will take a few weeks to a place called Chester. No one will look for us on the canal. You will be safe and can rest. Anna will get her strength back as she will need it in the times ahead. You and Anna have to stay on the boat during the day and only venture out in the evening or early morning when there are few people around. Once we get to Chester then you can find your way to Holyhead.

'I have a great deal of knowledge and skills to pass on to you. The journey will be like having school lessons but much more fun. Not many people like you have the gift and I am going to teach you how to use it for the good of others. We will start the lessons tomorrow after you have rested. Anna also needs rest and good food if she is to fully recover from the treatment she received.'

'Are you using magic to make things happen?'

Shelta laughed merrily. 'Magic only knows how to use the powers that once existed in all of us. Those powers could be used for good or bad purposes but we should only use them for good. Kindness, laughter and goodness are some of the most powerful weapons in the universe, but you will learn much of this over the next few weeks. Now that's enough explanation for today. Let's get rid of all your old clothing. I managed to get clothes that I thought would fit someone your size.'

Shelta stood up and gave her a clean plain white teeshirt and shorts, clean socks and trainers. Flo was surprised that the clothes and trainers fitted so well. She told Flo to snuggle back down under the blanket. She gently kissed her and made some strange gestures with her hands whispering, 'Blessed be.'

Flo's breathing slowed and soon she was asleep again. Anna was still curled up on the cabin floor and Shelta bent over her. She softly blew into Anna's nostrils and calmness flowed over Anna as she drifted off into a deeper sleep. She felt warm and safe for the first time in what seemed a lifetime since she had left her home.

The narrow boat cruised along the canals and every five miles or so, approached a lock. Shelta taught Flo how to open and shut the lock gates to allow the water levels to equalise between the lock and the canal. She explained to her exactly how, when the boat went into the lock chamber which had moveable gates at each end, that she had to open a valve which allowed the water from the canal to flow into or out from the lock, raising or lowering the boat. She said that you had to think of locks as a step-by-step way to move boats through water when the locks are at different heights. Flo thought that the system was very clever.

Anna had to stay below in the boat cabin during the day as Shelta did not want her to be visible in case word got back to their pursuers that a dog and a girl had been seen together. Flo took Anna out very early in the morning, when it was cold, or later in the evenings when it was quiet. Anna was very happy and felt so much healthier. Her coat was getting its shine back. She was noticeably putting on weight as well.

Shelta was so kind. Everyday she dressed in a new colour, often mixing reds and yellows with purples and browns. Her skirts billowed out behind her and she was just full of energy and laughter, often singing songs in a language that Flo didn't understand. When Flo asked her for the name, she simply said that it was the old language.

Flo was curious about everything and bombarded Shelta with questions about her life and her funny ways. There were so many strange items on the boat that she had never seen before but was somehow attracted to. Why did Shelta have a small dagger with runes carved into the handle? Shelta just laughed when Flo asked her about it.

After Flo had risen early one morning and taken Anna out for a small walk on the deserted towpath, Shelta told Flo that it was now time for her to start learning how to use her special talents.

'What do you mean, use my special talents?'

'You have been using your talents for healing without understanding them, just as you have been exploring the world of dreams and speaking to animals. A long time ago, we all had such abilities but over time, and for many other reasons, we stopped using them. We call this sort of knowledge, the Craft.

'The Craft has existed in every society in the world. Users of the Craft were once known as community doctors and they were experts in the use of herbs, oils, and healing. Some users interpreted dreams; others had visions about the future. They were respected and admired for their ability to use the earth, the trees, the stars, animals and all natural things for the purpose of good. The word 'Craft' means 'wise' and users have a close connection to Mother Nature.

'Over the years, users of the Craft have been persecuted and called witches and other names by those who sought to harm them. Of course, there are good and bad users of the Craft. Those who use it for power, greed or to do harm to a person are misusing the power they have. Those who use it to bring joy, pleasure, prosperity, love, and happiness into the lives of others are using positive energy.'

'So the Craft is magic?'

'Magic is spiritual power and is as natural in our lives as rain from the clouds. Magic is a tool to help you release the inner power within you. They are the same thing. There are different kinds of methods to learn about how to release the energy within you. You will find your own strengths on the path of life that you choose but the indications are that you have natural talents based on your nature.'

'What are those?'

'The ability for astral projection, which means that you can send your mind outside of your body; health-giving and interacting with the spirit world as well as channelling energies. I think that you also have a particular ability to communicate with animals which link to your ancestry.'

'Well I do see the old lady in my dreams who shows me things and seems to be a guide of some kind, and I know that I do speak to Anna without using words. Often I don't realise when I am doing it. It bothers me and makes me feel different from the other children. I have been very unhappy but Da always tries to cheer me up.'

'Everyone needs a guide to help them make sense of the world around them. Perhaps fate has sent you to me in order to be that guide. Everyday we will work together and I will help you understand the power that you have. Don't be afraid Flo, I will keep you safe. Already you have unlocked some powerful forces through your rescue of Anna. Your actions have been a good thing, even though now bad men are hunting you. No one can predict exactly what the future might bring but the most important principle of the Craft is that you must mind the threefold law when you seek to use it.' Shelta closed her eyes and began to chant,

'Mind the Threefold law
You should.
Three times bad
Three times good.'

'I don't understand what it means.'

'The moment you do harm to others in thought, word or deed, the law of karma, or fate, means that the harm will come back to you threefold. Similarly the good that you do will come back to you often in unexpected ways. You should not look for reward when you do a good deed. Doing well is a reward in itself.

'That's enough now. I've already given you so much new information to think about and your poor head must be bursting. But I have a task for you still. I want you to go for a walk. Leave the boat by yourself and just walk anywhere that you like. When you find a place which seems to be calm and peaceful, stop. Then you must look on the ground and pick up any object or items that you are attracted to.'

'How will I know where to walk? How will I know what to look for? It all seems silly. I could be walking for miles. How long do I walk for?'

'I can't answer your questions. You just have to trust me. You will find a special place and you will find special items that you feel strongly attracted to. Bring those items back to the boat. They will become lucky charms or talismans. Whenever you want to study and practice the Craft they need to be with you. These talismans will become more and more important in your life as your knowledge and skills develop. Now go and leave Anna here.'

The day Flo set off was bright and cold. The sky was piercingly blue and fluffy clouds hung in the air above her. She stepped on to the towpath and looked up and down the canal. She didn't usually go out in the afternoon but no-one was around. She couldn't make up her mind whether to turn left or right. She started to go left but her feet wanted to go right and so she turned and walked down the towpath. There was an opening in the hedge that ran along the side of the path. The small opening had thorns on either side and seemed forbidding but, following her intuition, she squeezed through, cutting her finger when she caught it on a big thorn. Her finger hurt and blood oozed out of the small hole that the thorn had made. She sucked her finger trying to stop the bleeding.

She froze, sensing that something or someone was close behind her. She heard panting. Even worse, something wet touched her hand. She stood as still as a statue slowly turning her head fearful of what she would see. It was Anna. She wondered why she hadn't sensed her but perhaps she had been concentrating on getting through the thorns.

'Anna, what are you doing here! We can't be seen out at this time of the day together. I'll have to take you back.'

Anna licked Flo's hand and sat down in front of her. She looked at Flo intently. Flo instantly knew that Anna would not leave her side.

She sighed. 'Alright, now you're here you might as well come with me but I don't even know where I'm going. I just felt that this is the right way.'

They walked forward and when Flo looked up, in front of her was an enormous oak tree. Its leaves spread in a thick canopy above the gnarled trunk and she imagined that she could see an old face carved into the centre. Anna walked slowly towards the tree and put one paw on the bark. Flo followed and put her own hand on to the tree. She had no idea what prompted her to speak to the tree, it seemed silly when she thought about it later.

'Please, Tree, keep Anna and me safe.'

She felt her hand grow warm and it seemed to tingle in a pleasant way. It was so peaceful and she looked at Anna who began scratching at the earth with her paws.

'What is Anna? What have you found?'

Anna started to dig with both paws and dirt flew up. Flo found a sharp twig and also began to dig, pulling the earth away with her other hand. After a short while they had dug a small hole which was about twelve centimetres deep. The roots of the tree wouldn't allow them to dig down any further. Flo saw nothing but earth, stones and a small worm. Anna stopped trying to dig and stood back from the hole. On impulse Flo put a hand down into the hole and continued to scoop the earth out its side. She suddenly stopped. Anna put a paw down into the hole and her claws scratched around a root near the bottom. She withdrew her paw.

Flo looked and saw a dull glint of something. She pushed both hands down the hole and scratched the earth using her fingers until she felt a round object.

'What's this? It's dirty but seems to be made of gold.' She spat on it and rubbed it until some of the dirt came off. 'I think that it is gold and it looks like there is snake on it.'

She held the small round disc in her hand and then put it carefully into her pocket. She remembered that Shelta had said that she should look around for anything that attracted her. She slowly walked around the tree but didn't feel an attraction to any item until she saw an old piece of oak, about ten centimetres long, lying near its base. She bent down and picked the stick up. Immediately she felt the same warmth and tingling in her hand that she had felt on touching the oak tree.

'What a strange stick. It's so smooth and look at the way it twists and turns almost like two snakes crossing over each other. It feels warm and tingly. Anyway, I think that I'll keep it. C'mon Anna, let's go back to the boat.'

Shelta was anxiously waiting for them. She gestured impatiently signalling that they must quickly get back onboard.

'Anna suddenly woke up, looked around for you and then jumped up the stairs and ran off on to the towpath. I couldn't stop her and decided not to try and chase her. What happened?'

Flo told her about Anna's sudden appearance and her experiences at the oak tree. She showed her the gold disc. Shelta carefully took it, washed it and then returned the disc to Flo.

'This is very old and has a design on the surface that I think I have seen before. It looks like a crowned serpent but I can't decipher the writing on the back of it. Perhaps there will be a clue in one of my books. I'll look later.' Shelta then rumbled around in one of her cupboards and came out with a gold chain which had links that looked like delicate leaves. The disc had a small hole at the top. Shelta tried to thread the chain through the hole and after some initial resistance, the tiny chain slid through the hole. She then placed the chain and disc around Flo's neck.

'I don't know exactly what this is Flo, it has something to do with wisdom, but I do know that it was meant to be found by you. Keep it safe. Don't take it off unless you feel that you have to. I think that it has some sort of charm woven into it. It really is very old.' Flo then showed her the stick that she had found and Shelta went silent for a time before speaking.

'This was also meant for you and is ancient. I sense great power in it. Don't give it to me. Put it away in your bag. I need to think and look at my books to see if I can find anything like it.'

She handed the stick back to Flo who put it away. It was now late afternoon. Flo felt exhausted and Anna was already back in her bed, head on her paws and sleeping. Shelta noticed that Flo had a faint mark on her finger and asked her what had happened. She just shrugged and said that she had caught it on a thorn and that it had bled a lot but when she looked closely at her finger, she saw that the cut was almost completely healed.

Anna dreamed. She thought of her family at home: her owner May, and the children, Lizzie, Eva and Alfie. She felt that she just had to return home soon. She had no idea what to do. Despite the warmth and love that Anna could feel flowing into her from Flo and Shelta, she still felt lost and lonely and something was stirring inside of her.

Flo was used to the motion of the boat by now. Time had simply stood still as the fugitives made their way along the network of canals stopping every few miles in order to pass through locks. She was getting really good at jumping off the boat, when Shelta felt that it was safe, and winding the mechanism which operated the lock gates allowing the water to swish in and out. Anna liked the sound that the water made. There was something very calming about being on the boat with Flo and Shelta. She could feel the joy of life growing within her at this special time even though she was fearful for the future. She knew that the stirring inside her meant that she was expecting puppies. Puppies that resulted from an unexpected encounter with a black Labrador some months ago.

She wanted to return home so that her puppies could be born in the house that she had lived in for so long. She could easily remember the smell of her owner, the children, her warm blanket and the thought of those smells made her feel happy. But her fate and future was now entirely in the hands of others. She thought about jumping off the boat and heading home by herself, but when she tried to determine the right direction to travel, she failed. There were just too many other strong scents confusing her.

Everyday Flo spent a short while sitting with Anna and speaking to her. She would close her eyes and try to link their minds. Sometimes she could clearly sense Anna's confusion and anxiety. The same thing happened to Anna. Flo's words made sense to her, linking to words that she already knew, but it was more of an emotional feeling that she felt. She too experienced Flo's anxiety and stress as she worried about the future. But they were making headway together. Flo became better at understanding both her emotions and needs. She understood that Anna was going to have puppies soon and that she wanted to be in her own home when they were born. She told Shelta who looked concerned, but didn't offer any advice.

Flo was also making real progress with the daily lessons that she was getting from Shelta and soaked up knowledge like a sponge. Shelta was a wise and kind person and she passed on her vast knowledge of herbs and their medicinal use. She also taught her how to meditate and focus her mind in order to achieve what she wanted. She taught her rituals that could help others, for example, how to find lost articles, how to achieve goals.

Most importantly, she helped Flo to understand how she could free her mind. Flo began to dream consciously, that is to say that she was aware that she was dreaming while dreaming. The feeling was such that she could see her body lying on the couch while she soared above it. It was a frightening feeling at first, but Shelta taught her how to master the technique so that she could move into levels of dreaming that previously were beyond her comprehension.

'Our dreams are wiser than our everyday minds and come from a source deep within us. Describe one of your dreams for me,' Shelta said.

Flo became thoughtful. She nearly always said 'Umm' when she spoke if she was thinking or was anxious. 'A huge wonderfully coloured butterfly with wings of bright blue and silver flew towards me in the last rays of warm sunlight at the end of a summer's day. I was walking in a meadow which was full of bright flowers of every description. White and yellow daisies mixed with red poppies and delicate blue and purple flowers that swayed gracefully in the light breeze. Huge yellow sunflowers with stalks over two metres high swayed and danced together. The butterfly hovered just above my head making me turn my face up to look at its beauty. I felt a light shining over me. Somehow I knew that the butterfly was the old lady who had previously appeared to me in my dreams and guided my actions.

'Then I saw a vision of me and Anna standing on the porch of a huge church which had light streaming through the windows behind us. We are lit up by a shaft of white light. Anna is sitting by my side. It is as if we are waiting for someone. The vision faded slowly leaving me bathed in a beautiful stream of golden light. When I opened my eyes my whole body was tingling and I felt full of energy. What did it mean?'

'Dreams are signposts. I think that you are to leave the boat soon. Perhaps the church has something to do with it. I really don't know. We finish our journey at Chester within two days. Chester is near Holyhead and the Irish Sea. You have to find your own way to Holyhead. You can probably get a lift in one of the many lorries that use the main road but perhaps that might not be the wisest thing to do. Burt and his men are still searching for a girl with a big dog and you will stand out. I have asked the Community to look out for you to take you to safety until we can let your Da know where you are. I will give you a secret word to say if you are approached and if the answer is correct, the person is a friend. If not, run.'

'I don't know Chester. What kind of place is it?'

'Chester is an old city originally founded as a Roman fortress. The city also has a cathedral which dominates the centre and is not too far away from the canal. In fact, I wonder if the cathedral is the church that you saw in your dream? Perhaps you should make your way there when you leave the boat. It is not far. Buses go from near there to Holyhead so you might be able to hop on a bus, even with Anna. That is all that I can do to help you Flo.'

Flo was really anxious about what would happen to her and Anna once they left Shelta's care and she communicated that anxiety to Anna. Anna could feel the puppies inside her beginning to stir. Her birth time couldn't be too far away and she knew that they were a long way from home and seemed to be going in the wrong direction as well.

Shelta was frightened for them but also knew that they had to continue their journey alone. Flo's dream gave her some confidence that all would be well, but she fretted anyway.

The boat finally moored in the canal near the centre of Chester. It was midday. The day was bright with a blue sky overhead but it was getting colder. Soon winter might set in. It was not a good season to be on the run. Shelta had prepared Flo's backpack and stuffed it full of food and drink. She had seen the oak stick that Flo had buried at the bottom of her bag but had not touched it. The stick radiated a power that almost forced Shelta's hand up and away as she tucked the goodies into the bag near old Ted.

The stick was still a mystery to Shelta and Flo had not wanted to use it in any of the rituals that had been taught to her. She just laughed and told Shelta that it was just an old stick. She dressed Flo like a boy with her baseball cap pulled down over her face and her hair hidden underneath. She wore her anorak and old blue jeans with grey trainers. The talisman that she had found under the oak tree hung around her neck and lay comfortably next to her skin. Flo said that the talisman always felt warm to the touch but that it wasn't the least scary even though it had a snake on it. Shelta had not been able to find what the inscription on the back meant even though she had spent hours looking through her books.

Flo said, 'We're ready,' although part of her didn't want to leave. She flung her arms around Shelta, hugging her so tightly. Shelta kissed her on the forehead and chanted words that she couldn't understand but they seemed to have a curious soothing rhythm. She made some signs in the air over Flo's and Anna's head. Kneeling on the floor of the boat beside Anna, she ran her hands along her belly feeling and exploring. She laughed loudly and hugged her, pulling an intricately woven rope over her head and handed the end to Flo.

'You can't let Anna run loose beside you or you will scare people, so she must be on a lead. But this is no ordinary rope and has spells of finding and safety woven into it to help keep her safe. It's the best that I can do.'

Anna felt excited. She jumped up from the floor, wagged her tail and then jumped up again putting both big paws on to Shelta's shoulders, giving her face a lick. Flo and Shelta laughed. It was time to go.

'I love you Shelta. You have been so kind to us and I feel that I have known you all my life. I have learned a lot but I know that I have only made a start. Sometimes I feel that I am drowning in knowledge.'

'There's iron in you girl. I believe that you have much to offer in life. I have loved looking after you and Anna towards the end of my own life and passing on what I know. You have been like a daughter to me. We may meet again one day, and I hope that it will come to pass, but until that day comes, remember the Craft law and always try to do good in a world full of bad.'

As they walked away from the boat, Flo turned her head and saw Shelta blowing kisses. It was a bittersweet moment and her eyes filled with tears. Anna suddenly stopped and turned her head looking back, before slowly carrying on.

Flo's spirits rose when she glimpsed the top of the cathedral. Perhaps, she thought, this really is the huge church that I have seen in my dreams. She felt excited but her excitement suddenly evaporated. Once again she had no real plan except to go to the church and wait. Flo knew that the plan might fail but it was all she had right now. She had to rely on her intuition.

Chapter Six

Sean was hiding. He had been forced to hide many times over the years and didn't like it. He knew that in the end, someone would always find you. You can hide but you can't run forever. His big problem was that he had no idea about the location of Flo and Anna but he could somehow sense that they were still safe and away from harm.

He knew that Mr Murphy would have sent Burt after them. Somehow he had to patch things up but he had no idea how to do this. He would need to speak to his friends and see if something could be done.

The site where Sean had been living near Holyhead over the past few weeks was owned by Mickey, one of his cousins. Mickey had hidden the old Land Rover and the caravan under tarpaulins alongside the other scrap cars that he bought and sold. Sean had been living in one of Mickey's old caravans on the site. He knew from his cousin that men were looking for him. There was a reward on his head.

Mickey had come up with a plan. 'I know a man called Fidgets who lives in Chester.

'Why is he called 'Fidgets?

'He drives you mad just looking at him. He can never keep any part of his body still, even for an instant. He's constantly on the move. But Fidgets owns a scrap yard, like me, and deals in stolen cars, caravans and anything that he can make a profit from. He owes me a big favour.'

'What did you do for him?'

'He's always in some sort of trouble and recently I gave him an alibi when he was arrested by the police for burglary. The thing is that sometimes he does get

genuine motorhomes which he fixes up and then sells
for a profit. If I can get him to take your Land Rover
and caravan in exchange for a motorhome, then we can
change the number plates and it will be hard to spot
you. You can find Flo and Anna and get the ferry to
Ireland.'

'I think that I've met him before. What's to stop
him giving me up to Mr Murphy? He's a thief and I
wouldn't trust him to keep his word.'

'Don't worry, he will do what I say. He owes me a
big favour. Also he won't want to upset you as he
knows about your reputation.'

'I still don't like it but go ahead and do the arrange-
ments. If he crosses me then he'll regret it!'

Mickey contacted Fidgets and had asked him to
take Sean's old Land Rover and caravan in exchange
for one of the motorhomes that he had in his yard. He
emphasised that the vehicle had to be legitimate and
not stolen. Fidgets told Mickey that he had just the
motorhome Sean was looking for. It was legitimate but
would need spraying white in order to smarten it up
a bit and was in need of a service. The interior was
fairly clean and big enough for a couple of people, even
one as big as Sean.

It was Sunday and Mickey arranged for Fidgets to
collect Sean's old transport the following week. Sean
could pick up the motorhome the next day at ten
o'clock. He said that once this was done, then the debt
Fidgets owed him would be fully repaid.

Sean arrived at the yard in Chester and found
Fidgets bent over the bonnet of a car. He straightened
up and hopped from one foot to the other.

'Hello Sean, how are you?'

'Is it ready?'

'Almost'.

'What do you mean? You told Mickey that it would
be ready this morning.'

'There's still some work to do after the respray.'

Fidgets was as thin as a rake, and smoked continually to such an extent that there seemed to be a permanent blue haze around his head. He wouldn't look Sean in the eyes but swivelled his neck nervously glancing at him slyly.

'You said it would be ready. You told Mickey that I was to come here at ten o'clock this morning and here I am. Mickey dropped me off. I want my wheels.'

'Steady Sean. No need to get angry. Just relax around the town for a few hours and I'll make sure that the boys finish it properly. You wouldn't want a half baked job now would you? We just had to do some other rushed work yesterday so couldn't finish your job, Calm down. Come back at four o'clock and it will be ready with a full tank. You can trust me Sean.'

Sean thought about it. Once he had the new transport he would head back to Holyhead and drive around looking for Flo and Anna. What else could he do? He felt sure that they hadn't arrived at Holyhead but were still on route. In fact he felt certain about it. The odds of finding them were stacked against him. He might be spotted by Mr Murphy's men before they could meet but he had to take a chance. He had beaten bad odds before. Luck could often be found when you most needed it. Sean wasn't a religious man, although he had been brought up in the Catholic faith, but he thought there was no harm in offering up a prayer for the safety of Flo and Anna.

'It had better be ready then Fidgets or you'll be sorry. I don't like being taken for a mug. Once you say something then make sure you mean it.'

'Look I'm sorry Sean, What more can I say? Just relax and go for a nice walk. When you come back you can drive it away.' Fidgets eyes flicked back and forth continually as his head bobbed about.

Sean grabbed him by his grubby shirt. 'Keep still

will you! I'm warning you, it had better be ready.' He
let go and turned around, walking towards the gate.

Sean left the yard and decided to go for a stroll down
by the canal. He liked water and thought that he
would be unnoticed on the canal path. He was worried
about Fidgets. He didn't trust him and if Fidgets had
discovered that Mr Murphy was after him, he knew
that he would reveal his whereabouts hoping to gain
favour with the boss man.

He shrugged his big shoulders, resigning himself to
fate knowing that he had no control over events. But
if Fidgets did betray him....

Sean liked to watch the narrow boats moving slowly
up and down the canal and thought that he and Flo
would enjoy living on one together. Perhaps on a boat
like that gaily painted narrow boat with the unusual
designs on its side, moored alongside the tow path by
the lock. He turned his head and saw the spire of the
Chester Cathedral towering over the town. A thought
struck him. He didn't want to wander aimlessly for the
next five hours so why not go to the cathedral, settle
down on one of the benches inside and have a snooze.
No one would find him there and he would be safe. He
could then slip back to the yard an hour early and see
if Fidgets was trying to trick him. He would be on the
lookout for any of Mr Murphy's men who might be
waiting for him. If things looked bad then he would
leave without picking up the motorhome and try to
think of something else.

He walked towards the cathedral. His feet seemed to
have a will of their own drawing him onwards and he
felt strangely calm and at peace with himself. He
approached the twin towers that dominated the
entrance to the west door of the cathedral and stopped
on the pavement, shading his eyes against the sudden
glare of light. He blinked, closed his eyes and then
opened them wide. Standing to the side of the main

doors was a young boy in a baseball cap with a dog
that he thought looked just like Anna. He closed his
eyes again and then reopened them. The pair were
still there. He felt his heart pounding and swallowed
nervously. Standing as still as a statue he watched in
disbelief as the boy ran towards him, arms thrown open
wide, with the dog bounding along by his side. The boy
was saying, 'Da,' over and over again.

Sean staggered backwards. Surely it couldn't be?
Then he saw the face of his lovely daughter. She was
crying, laughing and immediately grabbed him fiercely
around his arms as he bent down to hug her. Anna
jumped up and placed her paws near his shoulder and
licked his face. Tears of joy cascaded down Sean's
cheeks as in one motion he stood up lifting Flo high
into the air.

'Flo, it's you, really you,' cried Sean laughing as
more tears ran down his cheeks.

'Da, I knew we would be alright. Da, oh how I love
you and I've missed you so much.'

Flo's legs were now wrapped around Sean's waist as
she hugged him tightly. It seemed that everyone in the
street and in front of the cathedral had stopped to
watch the purest outburst of love and affection ever
made and time, for a moment, stood still as the sun
burst through the clouds sending shafts of brilliant
white light on to and around the cathedral. This
reunion was meant to be. Sean, Flo and Anna were
together at last. But a dark cloud still hung over them:
Mr Murphy and his men. Sean explained his plan to
Flo.

'I have to go back to Fidget's yard and watch what's
going on. I want to see if our motorhome is finished
and ready to go. I need to see if any of Murphy's men
are waiting for me which would mean that Fidgets
has betrayed me. I expect the worst but I won't do anything until dark. Once the place is locked up, then I

will break into the yard and take the motorhome.'

'It's so risky. What if they catch you? What will we do then?'

'They won't catch me. Once we get wheels we will drive to Mickey's place and change the number plates. Mickey has done the paperwork for the ferry to fool any checks at the port. The ferry departure from Holyhead to Dublin is a half past two in the morning and that gets us to Dublin by half past five so that we can be on the road early. But you're right Flo. If I'm not back by midnight then Mickey will come and look for you here. I have arranged to give him a signal if things don't go well for us. He will take you to safety but don't worry, I will be back for you.'

'What will we do once we get to Ireland? Burt and his men will still be looking for us.'

'I've contacted my cousin Frank who runs a travelling circus. The circus moves from town to town and is small but they are all good people and won't betray us. We'll be safe there for a while until I can sort out the problem with Murphy.'

'A circus! I love a circus and have always wanted to be part of one. Will they let me help out? Perhaps I could help with the animals? Anna will be safe there and could have her pups. I love this idea.'

Sean knew in his heart that much could go wrong with his plan but he spoke reassuringly to Flo in order to give her confidence. She accepted everything that he said and hugged reassuringly. She seemed to have an inner faith that was calming and radiated confidence, making Sean feel that he was doing the right thing.

'Right, now you and Anna have to stay around the cathedral near this road and try not to be noticed. After I get the motorhome from the yard I will come back for you. It will be dark. I will flash my lights three times which is the signal for you to come out of hiding and join me'.

Spirits were high between them even though Sean would soon be leaving. Flo tried not to think about what could go wrong and concentrated on what fun the circus might be. 'We're going to the circus Anna. You will be safe and perhaps even have your puppies there. Come on Anna, don't look so sad.'

Anna licked her hand as if to reassure her but she was still worried about her unborn pups and their safety and now they were going even further away from her home. She had a nagging feeling that there was big trouble ahead and Flo felt her discomfort.

Sean waited until early afternoon. He was near the yard well before the time that Fidgets had told him to return for the vehicle. He found a concealed position where he could see what was going on. His big hands held a pair of small but powerful binoculars, which he used when he was going horse racing. He could see that Fidgets had finished the motorhome. It was standing outside the garage and clearly had been sprayed white. There was no movement in the yard.

Sean looked around but still could see nothing that worried him. Suddenly he spotted a Land Rover parked in the road adjacent to the yard. He trained his binoculars on the vehicle and took in a deep breath. Sitting behind the steering wheel was Burt, and next to him was his side-kick Joe. Fidgets had betrayed him and contacted Mr Murphy! He felt his anger beginning to rise and clenched his fists. Fidgets would pay for this but not now. Sean's priority was to get the motorhome, change the old number plates, replace them with false ones and then get to the ferry. Now he would have to wait until dark in order to break into the yard.

He hoped that when he did not appear to pick up the motorhome, then Fidgets would tell Burt that he must have been suspicious about the collection and had changed his mind. He hoped that Burt would get bored after hearing this news and leave.

Darkness fell. Sean saw Fidgets lock up the garage and his men left work through the main gate. After an hour or so he saw Fidgets lock up the main gate and then casually walk around to the Land Rover knocking on the driver's side window.

'Where is he? You said that he would be here at four o'clock to pick it up. We've been waiting for over two hours. Where is he? Did you warn him off? If you did, then I'll give you to my dogs. Well....'

'N...n....no. Honestly I don't know where he is. He was supposed to come for the wheels. He said that he would. He had no reason to suspect that you would be here Burt. I didn't warn him and none of my lads did. He must have thought that something was wrong.'

'Suspected... or was told. If I find out later that it was you who spooked him then there won't be much left of you to bury.'

Sean saw a big hand grab hold of Fidgets and haul him towards the open window. Fidgets then staggered back into the road as if he had been hit in the face. The Land Rover roared into life and disappeared up the road in a cloud of black smoke. Fidgets held his head for a few moments, wiped his mouth with the back of his hand and quickly walked the other way. All was now quiet. There was nobody about and no cars on the road.

Sean waited a bit longer to make sure that it wasn't a trap. Nervously he walked up to the padlock and took out the bolt cutter which he had concealed in the large inside pocket of his overcoat. The cutter easily sheared the lock. Sean swung the gates open, stepped through them and closed them behind him before putting the broken lock back in place. He waited in the shadows for a few more minutes fearing a trap but no one came.

He quickly walked over to the motorhome and took

out a set of keys, trying different keys in the door lock until the lock finally opened. He sat in the driver's seat and again used his bunch of keys to find a key for the ignition. He turned the key to start the engine. The starter motor turned the engine over but the engine did not fire up. Sweat started to run down the side of his face. He tried again but nothing happened and it sounded as if no diesel fuel was getting into the engine. He wondered if Fidgets had sabotaged the engine.

Opening the bonnet he peered into the engine compartment looking for the diesel fuel pump. The light of his torch created shadows making it difficult to see. He could smell diesel fuel and so he knew that there must be diesel in the tank, but something was preventing it getting into the engine. Sean knew about engines. He wondered if Fidgets had put some sort of clip on to the fuel pipe to prevent the fuel from getting through. Sure enough, he saw exactly that. A clip squeezed the flexible fuel pipe. Sean seethed with anger but he knew that unless he calmed down, he would not be able to think clearly. He took a few deep breaths.

He worked his big hands down the side of the engine and managed to grasp the clip but he couldn't get his fingers around it. This was taking too long and he was worried about being discovered. He pushed his fingers down the side of the pipe once again, breaking the skin which started to bleed. Gritting his teeth he forced his fingers to push the ends of the clip together easing it back down the pipe. At last the clip was free. The clip slithered down the pipe releasing its tight grip. Sean thought that at least some fuel could now get through to the engine and he could cut the clip off later once he was away from the yard.

He jumped back up into the driver's seat. He turned the key. The starter motor turned the engine slowly over but did not fire. He tried again. His big frame

trembled as adrenaline coursed through his body.
There was a cough from the engine and then, reluctantly, it fired up although it ran raggedly. He put the
motorhome in gear but still left the lights off. He drove
slowly towards the closed gates. Leaving the engine
running, he jumped out and opened the gates widely
and then climbed back into the driver's seat. He slowly
drove forward keeping the lights off. Once through the
gates, he jumped down and closed them behind him
securing the padlock as best he could.

The engine coughed and sputtered as he threw
himself back into the drivers seat and he revved the
engine fearing that it would stop. He froze as the
headlights of a car swept down the road briefly
lighting up his vehicle but the car passed by. He
heaved a sigh of relief.

Switching on the lights, he crunched the gears and
moved off speeding up as he did so. That damned
engine. It was still coughing and spluttering and Sean
suspected that the clip that had slipped down the pipe,
was still preventing all the fuel from flowing into the
engine. He would have to take care of the problem as
soon as he picked up Flo and Anna. He hoped that he
wouldn't get stopped by the police on the way, or
worse, spotted by Mr Murphy's men.

Flo and Anna were waiting on the side road when
they saw the motorhome stop and flash its lights three
times. The passenger side door opened and they
jumped in. Sean was sweating in the driving seat and
said that they had to get out of town quickly but first
he had to fully fix the fuel pump. After a few minutes
working under the bonnet he jumped back into the
seat and started the engine which now ran well.

He laughed loudly with relief and Flo laughed with
him. Anna settled down to lie on the floor at Flo's feet.

'We're off to join the circus,' said Sean banging the
steering wheel with his fist. 'Here we go.'

Chapter Seven

Escape. They drove to Holyhead only stopping on the way to pick up the documentation and false plates for the motorhome provided by Mickey. Sean hid Anna in the rear of the motorhome covered with an old blanket. Under cover of darkness they arrived at the ferry terminal. Mickey had booked them on to the ship and both Sean and Flo had genuine Irish passports to show at the ferry booth. Their hearts were beating fast as so much could go wrong but to their great surprise, the sleepy woman in the booth just processed their documents, gave them a sticker for the lane that the motorhome needed to be in, and wished them a good journey.

To their relief the caravan in front of them was being towed by a big van with two hard looking men in the front. It was pulled over by Customs officers. Sean, however, was waved through and before they knew it, they were driving up the ferry ramp and parked on the deck.

Flo focused her mind on Anna, asking her to keep calm and sleep during the crossing but leaving her food and water to drink. She was worried that the motion of the ferry might upset Anna but there was nothing they could do about it. Anna was hidden from view in the back of the motorhome and Sean had checked that no one could see her from the outside. Flo and Sean were both on edge over the next hours worrying about her. Sean constantly looked at the other passengers to see if there was anyone that might be a danger to them.

In the event, the sea crossing to Dublin was calm and went without incident and, although they feared the worst, the fugitives left Dublin port without any further problem.

Once they were on the road, Sean began to relax and started to sing old Irish rebel songs in his deep voice which sounded a bit off key to Flo, but she was happy to see her Da in good spirits. They were driving up to the County of Roscommon, roughly in the centre of Ireland. One of its main towns was called Boyle. It was in Boyle that Sean had arranged to meet Frank who was master of one of the oldest circuses in Ireland: the Circus O'Donnell.

The first circus started in England in the 1700s and later, circuses had spread throughout the world, bringing laughter and pleasure to circus lovers everywhere. The Circus O'Donnell was a family affair and the circus was in the family blood. The family had strong links to the Community. Sean had shared many troubles over the years with the circus people and they helped each other out when needed.

Frank, the head of the circus family, was 65 years old. He was the Ringmaster. He was a tall slim man, powerfully built, with long arms. The muscles on his arms were like ropes. His face was long with a square chin and a strong nose. His brown eyes were sad but they would sometimes sparkle with mischief. He had had no formal education but his mind was as sharp as a razor and few men ever put one over him and got away with it.

When he was not working, he usually wore a smart green waistcoat which had silver threads woven into it, an open-necked white shirt with a green neckerchief knotted around his neck. He traced his family back to Donegal and was thought to come from a line of chiefs. He was a proud man and a natural leader of men. A born fighter and a man whom you would not cross without a second thought. He ran their small circus firmly but fairly.

His wife, Dareca, was five years younger than him and they had five boys and three girls. She was of medium height with a plump figure and was fond of wearing flowing coloured skirts with white blouses that showed off her ample bosom. She had seen and experienced great hardship in her life and yet her eyes were full of kindness and laughter.

Dareca was also not a woman to underestimate as behind her jolly plump face, which was framed by tumbling brown curls now showing some grey tips, was a will of steel. If she said it she meant it and all her children knew their place.

All the children had jobs and her eldest son, Anluan, his name meaning, 'great champion', was in charge of his siblings. Anluan managed the day to day running of the circus as well as its finances but he was a skilled equestrian and his speciality was trick riding on their two magnificent white Arabian horses.

Arabian horses had a history which went back over four and a half thousand years and were renowned for their ability to form good relationships with humans as well as being quick to learn and having great endurance. Anluan had a special relationship with his horses, just like Flo had with Anna, and seemed to be able to communicate with them without using words.

The circus act also had an airborne girl who could use the aerial rings to perform astonishing stunts; a contortionist called Gracie who could actually put her feet behind her head and walk like a spider. She seemed to be made of rubber. There were juggling acts, tumbling clowns, floor acrobatics, a magician who could make balls float in the air, a strong man who could bend an iron bar just using his neck and allow a car to be driven over him as he lay on a bed of six inch nails.

The performers would carry out mock battles using real swords reminding the audience of heroes of old.

They could all perform more than one act and were so versatile that it was hard to believe that you were watching the same person in a different role.

There were twenty five people in the circus, including the riggers who put up the big top. Many of the circus performers were married to each other and it was a very close knit community. The fugitives were warmly greeted on arrival.

'You're welcome here.' said Frank with a great smile on his face. 'I have a caravan for you and once you settle in, I'll introduce you to all the family.'

Everyone they met had a kind word for them and many already knew Sean. Anna quickly felt at home. No one asked questions about their troubles and they were treated as part of the family. Flo loved being there.

Circus life and travelling with the circus every day around the county of Sligo brought new experiences. They got to know all the performers and Flo became part of the magician's act, heavily disguised as a boy. The magician could do tricks that fooled the public using sleight of hand and hidden pockets but Flo found that she needed no trickery and astonished the magician when she made the silver balls that he juggled with, apparently float in the air by themselves without any effort. He demanded her secret but Flo just smiled at him and let the balls fall to the ground as if the trick had gone wrong.

Of course she kept her talents hidden except for her talent for healing which was much in demand. Everyday accidents happen in a circus. The animals get hurt and horses are especially vulnerable to damage to their legs from jumping. Anluan asked her to help with one of his horses. The horse had suddenly gone lame on its right leg and was limping. The farrier was perplexed and had tried all his skills to treat the horse. He was sceptical about Flo having the skills to help but Anluan insisted that she try.

'Let her have a look. What harm can it do? No disrespect intended to your own skills,' he said diplomatically.

'I've looked at her foot, shoes and lower limbs and can't find anything wrong with them. I can't find any trauma or infection but you can clearly see that she is distressed when she puts her foot down. I don't see how this girl could do more.'

'I don't know horses like you do, but I have been able to help heal a few in the past. Do you mind if I am alone with her for a while?'

'No, you go ahead. Take all the time you need, not that it will do any good.'

The farrier left her, accompanied by Anluan. Flo was alone in the stable with the horse. She stood in front of her and blew gently into her nostrils and then gave her a carrot. The horse's name was Sparkle and she had a lovely grey and white coat.

Flo spoke softly to her.' Can I touch your leg Sparkle? Will you let me?'

Sparkle whinnied and nuzzled Flo's neck. There seemed to be a bond between them and it was clear that Sparkle trusted her. Flo slowly bent down and ran her hands all the way down her front right leg letting her mind drift as she did so. Her hands seemed to feel inside the leg sending information back to her. She detected a decrease in energy flow at the back of the leg near the knee joint. Flo concentrated on that part of the leg visualising the healing process. She could feel heat radiating through her hands until she sensed a change in the energy flow. The flow became normal again. She slowly stood up and for one moment Flo and Sparkle were inexplicably linked and then the connection broke. Sparkle nuzzled her as Flo patted her flanks.

'I think that you will be better now but maybe you

shouldn't run for a bit until you feel that you really want to.'

Anluan and the farrier returned together with Dareca.

'Well, have you done your magic?' said the farrier sarcastically.

Flo ignored the jibe. 'Why not try a gentle walk with her and see how she goes?'

He took Sparkle out of her stable and watched her as she walked. She did not limp. He led her around in a circle and Sparkle walked in her usual balanced manner.

'It's impossible. I know that she couldn't walk properly and now I see with my own eyes that she can and she's in no pain. I just can't believe it and wouldn't have believed it unless I saw it myself.'

'I am glad that she is better and hope that we can be friends as I know that you didn't trust me but sometimes I can help. Not always though.'

'How do you heal the animals?' asked Dareca.'You have a real gift.'

'I see my energy as a river of silver sparking with life-force flowing into the injured part and revitalising each cell until that cell glows with health. If someone has a deep cut or broken skin I think that I will send into the wound an army of thousands of tiny soldiers all dressed in shiny armour and carrying the sharpest of swords. My army surrounds the enemy germs, dressed in black, and drives them from the wound leaving the wound ready to repair itself. I try to work with the body to heal itself. I can only tell you what I do. I don't actually really know how it works and I can't make broken bones whole again, but I seem to be able to speed up the healing process.'

Flo was embarrassed to have said so much about the subject but Dareca nodded and gave her a kiss on her forehead.

'You might not think that you are doing much, but
that is great power you have.'

Flo's reputation as a healer soon grew but Frank
told his group that no word of her powers should be
spread outside the company in case of wagging
tongues.

There was great joy in the circus. One evening Sean
told Flo to tell their story to the circus company. They
listened in wonder as Flo explained how she had come
to rescue Anna from Mr Murphy even against her Da's
wishes and the company gave her a hard look until
they saw Sean smiling and nodding for her to continue.
They all knew of Mr Murphy's reputation but nothing
was said.

Wise heads nodded when Flo described the journey
on the boat with Shelta. Dareca asked Flo many
questions about what Shelta had taught her and she
also asked to see the amulet that hung around Flo's
neck. She wouldn't touch it but said that she felt that
it was powerful. When Flo had finished telling their
story there was a general conversation about what was
needed to do next, especially as Mr Murphy would still
have his men looking for them. Frank told them not
to worry. He would work something out with Sean.

Before the shows Flo loved to watch the performers
practicing. They were all so talented but Anluan's
skills were simply astounding. Flo could sometimes
hear him talking to the horses as they galloped around
the ring and he performed back flips and other
amazing feats on them. He managed to do a handstand
with one hand on the back of both horses as they
jumped together over a small fence. How he stayed on,
was a mystery.

The circus was exciting and Flo loved every minute
of it joining in to help wherever she could. Sean stayed
in the background, often discussing plans late into the

night with Frank over a glass of whisky of course.

There were other dogs, male and female, that Anna got to know and they knew that she was expecting puppies and were kind to her. Anna was well fed and rested every day. Flo would take her for a walk around the circus tent early in the morning and evening when there were no strangers about.

Those were magical times and apart from Anna worrying about where her pups would be born and her strong desire to get home to her family, she felt very happy. If her puppies were to be born at the circus with people around her that were kind, and Flo was with her, then Anna would be content.

Frank and Sean discussed a plan to placate Mr Murphy.

'What do you think that I should do to get Murphy to back off and leave us alone, Frank?'

'He is a hard man to deal with no doubt about it and Flo took his dog. He couldn't care less about the dog but it will be all about his reputation. He will have to find you and Flo and make an example of you.'

'If he touches Flo then he will draw his last breath.'

'I know Sean but we have to be clever. He will want compensation for the trouble that you've caused him. Now I have done him a few favours in the past during the dark days and haven't asked for anything in return – yet. Now is the time for that. I also have some money set aside to offer as compensation. I will give it to you as Flo's fee for healing the horse and working with us.'

Sean protested.' I can't accept that Frank and you have sheltered us putting yourself at risk. I will pay you back, don't worry.'

'Well let's not fall out about it. At least we now have a plan.'

They shook hands and clinked glasses. Sean felt

good that he had such a friend as Frank by his side. Perhaps it would all work out for the best.

Christmas was fast approaching. The circus' last performance before the holiday was to be just outside Boyle near the old Abbey and the company arrived there on Wednesday in the early morning. The sky was bright blue and clouds drifted across, encouraging children to think about what shapes they made. It was cold with a promise of a fall in temperature later in the day when a fire in the hearth would be a welcome sight for some.

The last performance would be on Friday. The circus would perform over the weekend and then move on to their Christmas campsite to celebrate the festival. Some of the circus people would return home to their families across Ireland and there was a great feeling of anticipation of joy to come.

The circus had its own priest, Father Michael, who was a regular visitor and carried out births, marriages and arranged for funerals. Of short stature, he had the build of a bull and hands like shovels but the most startling thing about him was his eyes, deeply set beneath a heavy boned forehead, they were like whirlpools of intense blue. It was hard to hold his gaze for long and there was a sense of raw power within him. But he was a good man who took great joy in being the circus priest and the circus people loved him for it. He had arrived for the last performance of the year and met Flo, Sean and Anna. It seemed that he already knew a lot about them.

'I am very pleased to meet you both. Frank and Dareca have told me your story and I know that you must be worried about dealing with Mr Murphy. I know him from my days as a priest in Dublin. Not an easy man but at least you have a plan to put matters right. I will give you all the help I can. Remember we are not alone, we have God on our side.' He smiled and his infectious smile lit up his eyes giving him a mischievous look which made Sean and Flo smile too.

Posters had been put up all over Roscommon announcing the circus and the advance bookings were good. The Big Top would be full of adults and children who had come to enjoy the Christmas show. As usual, Sean's motorhome was parked at the back of the Big Top. Frank's men had disguised it by respraying it in a light grey colour. Anna usually slept underneath the motorhome on a snuggly old blanket unless it was wet and rainy, in which case she would sleep next to Flo on the caravan floor.

The Friday night performance came. The Big Top was full. All the performers were inside ready to delight the children and adults. It was always an exciting time. Sean would help the riggers put up the equipment and Flo was doing more and more tricks, dressed as a boy, helping the magician.

Anna lay on her blanket with her head poking out from underneath the motorhome listening to the sounds of the circus. It was cold and Flo had put an extra blanket over her to keep her warm. As night came down, the lights illuminated the circus tent, casting shadows everywhere. Anna was dreaming, warm, happy and content, transported far away to a pleasant place. But life can change in a heartbeat and it did.

Burt and Joe had not been idle. The next day, after they had found out that the motorhome had been taken from the yard, they suspected that Sean would head for Ireland. They had let it be known on Mr Murphy's network in the underworld that there was a reward for information which led to the discovery of the fugitives. But somehow their prey had escaped them and Burt was furious.

Eventually Mr Murphy received information that Sean was travelling with the Circus O'Donnell and he had relayed this to Burt and Joe. His informers had tracked down the circus to Boyle, in Roscommon.

'Now listen carefully you two idiots. Once you find Anna you are to only snatch her. Don't bother with the girl. Bring the dog back safely to the yard at Mudchute. When we have her, I know that Sean and the girl will have to return to try to get her back. That will cost them dearly.' He paused in thought. 'Now remember, this will be your Christmas present to me and if you fail, I have a very interesting Christmas present for both of you.' Mr Murphy smiled but there was no humour in the smile.

Burt and Joe were exhausted. They knew that they couldn't fail. For days they had been watching the circus from a raised viewpoint sitting in a borrowed old farm lorry which would not look out of place when it was parked nearby. They couldn't stay in the town as word would soon get to the circus that they were looking for someone, and locals didn't like strangers. Burt knew that the last performance would be that very evening. Anna would be in her usual place. It was time to strike. He took out the tranquilliser gun that he had brought with him and gave it to Joe.

'Listen Joe, once they are all inside the Big Top and Anna is unguarded, you have to creep up on her and shoot her with the gun. Then pick her up and bring her back to the lorry. We'll drive up the road, throw her into the cage in the back of the Land Rover, and make the ferry but only if we get a move on. Got it? Don't muck this up. Now get going.'

Burt pushed him sideways towards the door. Joe nodded. He didn't like this dirty business with Anna but he had to do as Burt said. He knew that Mr Murphy would not be pleased if the job was botched. He sighed heavily and got out of the lorry concealing the tranquilliser gun underneath his coat. He made his way slowly towards the circus. He crept around the back of the Big Top. It was dark but there was just enough light from the moon to see his footing and he quickly made out the shape of the motorhome. Creeping behind it on his hands and knees, he looked underneath and saw that Anna was sleeping peacefully on her old blanket. Once again his conscience pricked him as he knew that once Anna was in Burt's hands, her world would collapse but what could he do?

He wriggled forward on the wet grass and lay still. Now he could see Anna's back only a few metres away from him. Carefully he removed the tranquilliser gun from his pocket and took aim. Anna began to come out of her dream sensing that something was wrong. She sniffed the air and the smell of Joe hit her senses, stunning her momentarily.

She tried to stand up and turn towards him but heard a crack and felt a sharp pain at the back of her neck. She growled and continued to turn but her legs felt like rubber and they started to collapse underneath her. Her head felt fuzzy and she was confused. The last thing that she remembered was sinking down and down until there was only blackness.

Joe saw Anna collapse and wriggled out from his position putting the gun back into his coat pocket. He stood up and edged his way around to the front of the motorhome. There was nobody about. He heard clapping and loud music coming from the Big Top. He grabbed hold of the edges of Anna's blanket and pulled it forward. Anna was a dead weight and he had difficulty sliding it along.

He suddenly saw bulges in Anna's belly. He realised that she was pregnant and his conscience pricked him again knowing that Burt would love it when he found this out. Not for any good reason. He rolled Anna back into her blanket, bent down and lifted her onto his

skinny shoulders. Joe was wiry and very strong and so
he made light work of her weight. Moving carefully up
the road unnoticed, he joined Burt back in the lorry.
Burt laughed when he saw Anna.

'Gotcha,' he said gleefully. 'Gotcha.'

He drove the lorry to the concealed Land Rover
and together they transferred Anna, putting her into
the hated cage. She was sound asleep and breathing
very slowly. Burt crashed the gears as they set off,
whistling happily to himself. Joe sat in the passenger
seat staring at his boots and wishing that he hadn't
been involved in the snatch but it was much too late
for regrets.

'The dog has enough tranquilliser to keep her down
until we get back to Mudchute so we won't have any
trouble on the ferry. It doesn't matter what condition
she is in anyway,' said Burt grinning.

'She's with pups,' said Joe, 'and Mr Murphy is going
to want to sell those pups so we had better see that she
doesn't die on the way back,'

'Pups! Pups!' roared Burt. 'Even better. The girl will
know that and so will Sean. They will have to come
back for her now. Pups! Pups! Mr Murphy will be
pleased. We may just drag ourselves out of the fire
with this. Are we going to have some *fun*?'

Joe's face was miserable as he looked back at Anna
lying, as if dead, in the cage. He knew what Burt's idea
of fun was.

Chapter Eight

Flo's joy from the success of the evening instantly turned into despair. She felt a stabbing pain deep inside her head almost at the same time that Joe shot the tranquilliser dart into Anna. She knew that something was badly wrong and she ran to find her Da. He was talking and laughing with one of the tent riggers near the entrance of the tent but stopped the minute he saw Flo running towards him.

'What's wrong Flo?' asked Sean, his voice cracking with strain.

'It's Anna. Something has happened to her. I felt a shock run through me just minutes ago. I know something bad has happened. I just know it.' Her face crumpled into tears and she clenched her little fists. 'Come on Da, we must see what's happened.' She frantically pulled on the front of his coat.

Turning his big frame towards the circus entrance he began to run. Flo and some of the riggers followed him as fast as they could, approaching the motorhome which was in shadow. Laughter, clapping and exclamations of wonder at the feats which the audience were experiencing exploded out of the tent as the show came to a close. But there was no sign of Anna. Flo crawled underneath the vehicle and looked at Anna's crumpled blanket. There was a strange medicinal smell in the air and she snatched the blanket and smelled it. Sean grabbed it from her and did the same.

'Tranquilliser.' He flung the blanket to the floor in disgust. Tears flooded down Flo's face as she stood up beside him. The future had looked so bright, the worst behind them. She was stunned at how quickly her world had been turned upside down.

'They've taken her, they've taken her. Burt has snatched her and they are taking her back to Mr Murphy. They will hurt her. What's going to happen to her puppies now?' She sank slowly down to the ground, holding her head in misery.

Word about the kidnapping had passed quickly through the circus community and already a crowd gathered outside their motorhome now that the show was over. Angry voices buzzed in the background and there was tension in the air.

Frank, resplendent in his Ringmaster's outfit, and Dareca came hurrying through the crowd and stopped beside Sean. Frank's face was creased with lines of worry.

'What's the matter?'

'Anna has been snatched by Murphy's gang. Most likely they've taken her back to Mudchute. They know that we will come looking for her. Murphy wants his pound of flesh.' Sean clenched his fists.

'We need to act quickly if we are to save Anna,' said Dareca, her eyes bright and her brain whirring with possibilities. 'Frank, get Father Michael and the boys and tell them to meet us back at our caravan. We'll join you in a minute.'

Dareca tenderly pulled Flo up from the floor and cuddled her. She put her hand, heavy with rings and bracelets, under Flo's chin and raised her head up until she was looking directly into her eyes.

'Flo, now listen to me. No one hurts our family and gets away with it. You are family. We will get Anna back for you. Whatever it takes. I promise you.'

Flo put her arms around Dareca and buried her head into her body feeling the warmth and love that came to her. She stopped crying. Her face was grim with determination.

'If Murphy's men harm Anna then I will spend the

rest of my life hating him. He will never rest easy with me. I will do everything that I know to hurt him.' She spat this out with such fury that Dareca felt that she had been almost physically struck by her words and that Flo's hatred had become a force that could be touched.

She stroked Flo's hair and spoke softly to her.

'Flo, I understand that you are hurt and that you seek revenge but you must understand that evil deeds will come back to haunt you for the rest of your life. Revenge will eat into your heart and poison you. The Chinese have a saying: if you seek revenge then dig two graves. This means that nothing good will come from a life dedicated to hatred. You are not made for hatred. You are made for love and it is your love of Anna that is important not your hatred of Murphy. Now we will make a plan. Dry your tears and just think of the love that you have for Anna. Send her that love. I know that you can. Let Anna know that you will come for her so that in her darkest hours she will find some comfort.'

Flo felt much calmer under the influence of these wise words but she was also certain that nothing would stop her from returning to Mudchute and trying to get Anna back. She reached out to Anna, as Dareca had suggested, and sent love towards her. Somewhere in her drugged mind Anna felt that love wash over her as once again she lay alone and miserable in the darkness. A bright spark danced in Anna's mind giving warmth and comfort. Flo had sent Anna something that was beyond price: hope.

Frank's large comfortable caravan was crowded. There was standing room only. Frank looked at the assembly: Sean sat on the sofa almost taking up its entire length; Dareca sat beside him squeezed up at the end and Flo sat on the edge of one of the arms, dangling her feet. Anluan lounged against the sink looking relaxed but coiled for action like a big cat. His brothers were near him. Father Michael was seated at the table next to Frank. Father Michael was short but his wide shoulders clearly showed him to be a man who relished physical activity. His black jacket seemed to be straining at the seams and his neck was just about encircled by his white dog collar, the symbol of his priesthood. He had a large open face with ruddy skin and looked much younger than his sixty years of age. Normally his blue eyes twinkled with good humour but they held a steely look now. He had seen much in his life. Almost too much for one man to carry alone.

A priest is the conscience of his flock but must hold dark secrets locked away forever in his mind. Every week he has to hear confessions that often reflect the worst of humanity when parishioners pour out their sins, seeking absolution. The penitent can walk away feeling lighter because of the confession but the priest must then take on the burden of knowledge.

Father Michael was a good man. He loved God and believed that good could overcome evil in all its forms, but there was always a price to pay. He loved the circus and circus people but why he did so was a complete mystery even to him. He just felt drawn to that life and over the years had become an important part of Frank's family. Yet despite his love for the circus Father Michael had to administer a parish in a very rough part of Dublin where daily he saw lives ruined by drugs, alcohol and violence. His work in the parish had brought him into contact with Mr Murphy and some of his associates. He knew that Mr Murphy was not a man to be treated lightly, and the fact that he had arranged for Anna to be snatched meant that he was very angry. Mr Murphy had only one way of dealing with those that crossed him and that was to hurt them.

Father Michael had a fierce intelligence and he resonated calm but shades of the street fighter could emerge when grappling with a local problem. Now his mind was furiously working on a plan of action but in his heart he thought that, unless God intervened in some unknown way, Anna might be lost to Flo forever.

Frank opened the meeting. 'We all know why we're here. Murphy has Anna. He wants Sean and Flo to go back and beg for her. He probably wants big money as compensation for stealing the dog in the first place.' Flo began to protest about this but Dareca stopped her with a sharp look. 'Murphy has crossed the line with my family and that means trouble for him as well. It may mean breaking heads but I mean to get the dog back.' Frank almost shouted out his last sentence and the atmosphere in the caravan thickened as fists clenched and sinews hardened. Sean's eyes bulged and he shifted his weight on the sofa.

It was Father Michael who spoke next in a soft, yet compelling voice. 'Before we talk of hurt let us all pray for a moment. Pray to heal the hurt that Flo has had by the loss of Anna. Pray for Anna and her unborn pups but most of all, pray for Mr Murphy and those that snatched Anna, that they will see the light when lost in the darkness of evil.'

Father Michael said a short prayer and the atmosphere in the caravan became less tense. Even Flo felt calmer now that he was there and his voice seemed to reach out to her.

'We must go to see Mr Murphy,' he said, 'but just a few of us should go. I know him from Dublin and maybe I can persuade him to end his vendetta against Sean and Flo and we can get Anna back. We might need to compensate him for his trouble.'

Frank had been listening closely and now looked at Dareca who nodded in his direction.

'I'll front the money. Not a bother Sean. We agreed.

You can pay me back when you have it if you want. No arguments, this is family business.'

Sean held Frank's gaze for what seemed an eternity but then slowly nodded his head mumbling his thanks. Flo's heart fluttered at this generosity and she looked at Dareca who smiled.

'That's settled,' said Father Michael, 'I will go back with Sean and Flo. No need for you all to come. We don't want a war with him but we have the promise of compensation and Murphy does owe me a favour or two which I think that I can call in. He's not an easy man to deal with.' Frank began to protest but Father Michael held up a warning hand while looking at Dareca and his eyes swivelled around to where the boys were standing. 'You all know that there will be fighting if we go mob-handed so please let me handle it. If I fail then we can do it the hard way but please God, I won't fail.' Father Michael said this with great confidence and in such a strong and powerful voice that the whole of the caravan was silent.

Father Michael's hand dropped into his jacket pocket and his fingers tightened on the cold metal which he turned over in his pocket. The heads began to nod in agreement, some more reluctantly than others as the youngsters were up for fighting. All eyes turned on Frank. He would have the final say. He stood up from the table and looked around. His hawk-like eyes then rested on Father Michael. His voice was strong and clear, a leader of men.

'Father Michael, Sean and Flo will go. If the business is not settled within the week then I will take charge, No arguments.'

And so the rescue party with Flo, her Da, and Father Michael left for Mudchute with all the love and best wishes that the Circus O'Donnell could give them. They had a plan, but in their hearts they knew that it might fail. No one wanted the violence which would come if the plan did fail. They had to act quickly.

Anna was back. The big Land Rover rolled into the yard and the smell of that place and the pain that Anna had previously suffered flooded her senses. She trembled as she thought about Burt and his evil collar. Her puppies moved restlessly inside her as if they too could feel their mother's fear. The smell of fish from the nearby market hung in the air and Anna had a flashing memory of the crab that hung on to her tail in the back of that dark smelly lorry. So much had happened since then.

The back door of the Land Rover opened and Joe stood there.

'Come on Anna, I won't hurt you but you have to go back to your cage so no trouble now.'

Trouble? Anna was weak and shaky and still groggy from the effects of the drug. She could hardly stand up after being thrown about in the back of the Land Rover. Slowly she got up from the floor, flattening her ears and trying to look submissive. Joe slipped a chain attached to a lead over her head and pulled her forward. She tried to jump down from the back of the Land Rover but fell on to the dirt. With a great effort she got to her feet and wagged her tail to show that she meant no harm. Joe gently led her towards the cage, whispering encouragement to her in a kind voice.

'Stop!' Anna turned her head and saw Burt moving towards them. 'I said, "Stop".' Burt held the hated black collar in his hand. 'Put this on her, Joe, and she'll be as good as gold, won't you Anna?' said Burt with a look of hatred in his eyes. Burt seemed like a predator that wanted to kill her and once again fear coursed through her body making her shake and tremble.

'She doesn't need that, Burt, she can hardly stand up now. She ain't going to be no trouble Burt. Leave her to me.'

But Burt stepped forward and grabbed Anna by the scruff of her neck, leaving on the chain but adding the hateful black collar. His face was so close to Anna that she could have bitten him. The smell of decay came off from his huge body and she tried to shrink away. Burt let go of her and stepped back holding the black box in his hand. Anna could see the red light glowing on it. She knew what was coming next.

'Don't hurt her, Burt. Mr Murphy will go crazy if you kill her and those puppies don't get born. He wants them. He already knows how much he can get for them. We need the dog to be healthy, not dead.'

Burt looked at him giving a hard stare but took his hand away from the box.

'Maybe you're right, but once these puppies are weaned, she's mine to do what I like with. Understand!' He turned quickly and walked away leaving Anna with Joe who led her back to her cage.

Joe gently stroked Anna's head and she licked his hand to show that she meant him no harm. Perhaps he would help her. There were no other dogs in the nearby cages and the old smells told Anna that they had not been used for some time. She wondered what had happened to all the dogs and feared the worst. She lay down on the floor of the cage. Joe locked the cage and went away, soon returning with food and water for her which she gratefully gobbled up.

Her thoughts then turned to Flo. Where was she? She felt that Flo was trying to reach out to her and send her comfort but her mind was full of fear and emotion and she found it difficult to concentrate on good feelings. As she lay in the bottom of the cage it was so hard to feel hope and the picture of Burt and his box kept surfacing.

Mr Murphy sat in his office upstairs. He knew that

Burt and Joe had snatched Anna and brought her back. In fact Mr Murphy didn't need Anna any more as he had left the security dog business and had sold off the other dogs. He could make better money elsewhere. The security business was too much trouble. He had enough guard dogs to protect his premises and could always get more if he needed them.

He would have to get rid of Burt and Joe now their job was done and he had Anna back. They were no further use to him and firing them would save him money. He didn't much like Burt anyway but he had been a good dog trainer, if a bit too heavy handed from time to time.

Mr Murphy liked the idea that Anna's unborn pups could be sold for a good profit. He knew that Sean would come back with his girl running after the dog. He snorted. Sean was too soft. A big man with a soft heart. Useless in shady business and easy to manipulate once you knew his weakness. He expected that when Sean came back that he would try to offer compensation for the trouble the girl had caused. He, however, had no intention of taking the money although he would play with Sean first setting a sum for Anna's return which he knew that he couldn't match. No, he had another plan and one that Sean wouldn't expect. Yes, the more he thought about it the better he liked it. He smiled. He really liked it when he knew that he had someone wriggling on his hook. No one took anything from him without a pay-back. In the underworld it was the law of the jungle. You earned respect through fear. Sean could wriggle but he would never get off the hook.

Mr Murphy liked respect. Respect through fear. Fear that if a man crossed you there would always be pay-back and that usually meant someone got hurt, and hurt badly. He smiled again at the thought.

Suddenly he clutched his head and the pain in his

skull seemed to explode with ferocity. The headaches were getting worse and the quacks were useless. Despite all the tests, no doctor had been able to find out why he was getting them and yet everyday, without warning, he suffered. Only whisky seemed to dull the pain but whisky made him mean. He reached for the bottle that he always kept handy in his drawer and poured himself a large glass. drinking it down in one gulp. The whisky hit his system and the pain in his head dulled leaving an intense throbbing behind his eyes which he knew would last for at least one hour or maybe even more. His vision suddenly blurred and bright diamond shapes danced in his eyes until he had to close them to shut out the light which seemed to increase the pain in his head. He lowered his head on to his desk and covered it with his arms as if trying to hide away from the pain and the world. But the agony was terrible and in fact became so bad that he repeatedly banged the desk with his fist as if attacking it would make the pain go away but the pain got worse.

Anna raised her head and sniffed the air. The same horrible smells floated across her nose. But her head was clearing and she felt that Flo was trying to make contact with her, calling her name. She suddenly felt a warmth flood through her. Her puppies seemed excited as well and she could feel them moving inside her. Flo was coming. She could not be far away and her presence was getting stronger. She felt hope. Flo would surely rescue her. She stood up in her cage and felt herself growing stronger. There was nothing to do but wait and she watched the yard carefully but there was no sign of any activity.

In fact Anna was right. The rescuers were not far from Mudchute. Their journey had been uneventful with Father Michael telling them about his life as a priest. He had them laughing at times, which was his intention, as he tried to take their minds off the task ahead. He sensed that Flo was no ordinary girl and asked her about her life. He asked her in such a kind way that she almost felt compelled to tell him every detail, including her journey with Shelta and what she had learned from her.

'You know Flo, there is a place in God's world for everyone and as long as you mean good, and not harm, you can live a full and meaningful life. Perhaps you have been given the powers that you have for a higher purpose. What is that around your neck?' Flo told him that Shelta thought that it was a very old talisman, meant to be found by her. 'I'm interested that you seem to be able to send your spirit outside your body. Is that true?'

'Yes. I can't do it at will quite yet but I am getting better at controlling my flights. Sometimes I am able to fly in a way that is so real that I am not sure if I am dreaming. I searched for Anna when I was on the crossing and found her at Mudchute. She is scared and so I sent her comfort. She knows that we are on the way. Please tell me again about the plan.'

'We have about two thousand pounds to offer Mr Murphy as compensation for you taking the dog. It is all we have but I think that I have a card up my sleeve that might swing the deal for us.'

'What is it?'

'I prefer not to say at this stage. I want to see how he reacts to the offer of compensation first.'

'What can we do if he doesn't want money and your card doesn't work?

'It is in God's hands Flo. Only he knows what will happen but we can only do our best,'

Finally their car arrived at the gates of the yard. The gates were open. There was no sign of life. The rescuers drove into the yard and Flo immediately saw Anna.

'Anna, Anna,' she shouted, 'we're coming for you.'

Flo jumped out of the car even before it had come to a halt and ran towards Anna's cage. Anna barked excitingly and did her best to move about in the cage pawing the bars as if she could tear them apart. The door of the shed was flung open with a crash and Burt ran out with Joe not far behind him. He spotted the car and saw Sean and Father Michael straight away. They were trying to get out of the car and Sean was struggling as his weight was pulling him back into the seat. Burt moved fast for a big man, ran across the yard and grabbed Flo lifting her easily off the floor.

'Not so fast, dog thief, not so fast,' he sneered.

His face was inches from Flo and his horrible breath made Flo feel sick as she dangled in his huge fleshy arms. Sean was out of the car now and starting to move quickly towards Burt intent on knocking him down when Father Michael restrained him by putting his arm, which felt like an iron bar, in front of Sean's face.

'No Sean, not that way or we will never have a chance to get Anna back.'

'Put Flo down Burt,' said Sean through gritted teeth, 'put her down now. It's your boss that we want to see. Put her down.'

Burt slowly lowered Flo to the ground still holding her by the arm.

'No one goes near that dog until Mr Murphy says so,' Burt scowled. He released Flo and pointed his finger at her face. 'That includes you, you little thief.' He stood still in front of Anna's cage and folded his arms. His eyes, which were usually hidden under his drooping eyelids, bulged as he glared at Flo.

'Flo come over here,' said Father Michael who still had his hand in front of Sean, restraining him, 'we need to sort this out with Mr Murphy not with Burt.'

Burt laughed. 'Yes, sort it out if you can, priest, but

that dog is mine once the puppies are born. Anyhow, a priest won't make a scrap of difference to Mr Murphy I can tell you. You might as well get back in the car and run back to your Irish bog,' he snorted. He walked casually over to Anna's cage and looked at her. He kicked the cage with his boot and Anna fell over onto her side hitting the bars. She yelped in pain as one of the bars caught her paw as she fell and ripped her nail. Flo threw her hands up across her face in horror and she could feel Anna's fear coursing through her. Burt turned, faced the rescuers and slowly smiled. 'She's mine and there's nothing you can do about it.' He kicked the cage again.

The shadows in Mr Murphy's bare office created dark corners despite the daylight which was filtering in. He had just one desk lamp turned on which cast a pale eerie light around the room. It may have been the dim light that had changed his appearance as he seemed to have aged considerably and his once straight frame was slightly bent. Pain can do that. He had been watching events from his window looking down at the rescuers in the yard. Even he had clenched his fist when Burt had kicked Anna's cage and he had felt inexplicably annoyed at this stupid violence. Mr Murphy never hurt anyone needlessly. He paced up and down the room. He felt exhausted and his usually agile mind seemed full of cotton wool. He rubbed his temples and a feeling of intense depression came over him like a dark cloud. He winced at the memory of the searing pain that he had felt on waking up in the morning. His head had felt that it would burst. It was agony and even the large whisky and pain killers that he had gulped down only partially dulled the pain. He thought about his actions. Of course I was right to send Burt and Joe to get Anna back. The girl stole my dog and her Da helped her. Worse, they had hidden themselves with Frank in his stupid circus.

I couldn't care less about Anna although strangely
for me, I didn't like it when Burt had kicked her cage.
I do care about my reputation. If someone in my world
thought that I was going soft then my empire could
fall apart. My reputation for being a hard man has
kept them all in line. No-one crosses me, even for a
stupid dog. I like Sean. Weak, but he is a good man to
have about. Still, I have to teach him a lesson and that
lesson will be like throwing a pebble into a pond. Once
word gets out of what I have done to him, it will shock
even the lowlife that I have to deal with. What about
that priest? He knows that I owe him a favour but he
thinks that he can collect on it. I never really liked him
anyway. Always meddling in my affairs in Dublin and
trying to do good. Yes I owe him a favour but all that
means is that I give a hefty donation to the Church
and the Bishop will be pleased. Stupid to have come all
this way for nothing. As for the church, they always
seem to prize money above faith. If there is a God, why
doesn't he stop these damn headaches? That priest can
plead all he likes to get Anna back. He might as well
be talking to stone when it comes to business and
Anna is my possession. They won't like what they have
to do if they want her back.

Mr Murphy opened the door to his upstairs office.
The rescuers looked up at him standing still like a
statue. His voice was soft yet full of menace.

'Get in here, all of you.' He let the door shut with a
bang as he disappeared back inside.

Burt and Joe hurried forward and Burt's heavy boots
banged on the metal steps as he wheezed his way up
with Joe trailing closely behind. Father Michael, Sean
and Flo followed.

'Leave the talking to me,' Father Michael said in a
low voice, touching the cold metal in his pocket.

They entered Mr Murphy's office. There were no
chairs to sit on. He was seated in his swivel chair. He

looked up at the ceiling. You could have heard a pin
drop. Suddenly in a flash he spun around and banged
the table so hard with his fist that the lamp jumped
into the air and almost fell off. All those in the room
took a step back in alarm and Flo flung her hands up
to her face in surprise. His teeth bared in a grin that
had no laughter in it.

'You took my dog. Explain.'

Father Michael began to open his mouth to reply
but Mr Murphy held up his hand in warning.

'Not you. The girl.'

Flo took a small step forward feeling small and
timid. Her hands went up to the medallion around her
neck and unexpected warmth began to flow through
her. It seemed as if invisible energy was powering her
body and that each cell had suddenly come alive. She
closed her eyes for a moment and instead of feeling
small and timid, she felt strong and powerful. Powerful
beyond her years. Her mind reached out and locked
with Mr Murphy's.

Instantly she experienced the rage, hate and pain
that he was feeling as if she had been physically
struck with a hammer. She let out an involuntary cry
and staggered back nearing falling to the ground but
once again she felt the power of the medallion calming
and soothing her. When she opened her eyes she saw
that Mr Murphy had stood up and was gazing intently
at her. He was back in control. He pointed at Flo.

'I want you. You will come and work for me to pay
for stealing the dog. You can act as a go between for
my deals. Children can move about freely in the cities
and if you get caught by the police, nothing much will
happen. Anna will have her puppies. I will sell them for
a good profit. You can keep the damn dog if you want
to but you stay with me.'

When he heard this, Burt took a step forward.

'You said that I could do what I liked with the dog,'

he spluttered.

Mr Murphy spat out the words in a low threatening voice.

'You're fired. You and Joe. I don't need you. I've shut down the business. Now get out of my sight. Get out now.'

Burt and Joe stumbled backwards fearing that in this dark and dangerous mood that he might even shoot them there and then if they didn't do as he said. Burt opened the office door, clattering back down the stairs into the yard. Joe almost fell down the stairs behind him.

Mr Murphy sat down. The room was silent. Flo was still holding her medallion; Sean was breathing heavily and red with rage. He bunched his big fists. Father Michael began to speak. Mr Murphy quickly put up his hand once again to stop him.

'I'll give money to your Bishop so that it pays off any past favours that you've done me. Your business is finished here. Get out.'

Sean had had enough. He had been silent but inside he was like a volcano ready to explode. Nobody would take his Flo. He would rather die first and he wasn't afraid of Murphy. Now was the time for action. He thrust his head forward. He was ready. Murphy was for hell. Father Michael moved in front of Sean, blocking his forward motion. The priest slowly reached into his pocket and touched the cold metal there. Mr Murphy's hand suddenly snaked out from beneath the desk as he pointed a gun straight at him. No one moved. The air boiled with tension.

'Put the gun away Pat. You don't need it and I have no gun myself. Let me take my hand out of my pocket and give you a gift. Put the gun down Pat.'

Mr Murphy slowly lowered the gun and placed it on the table in front of him. He still had his hand on the trigger.

'Show me your hand and slowly now. I wouldn't want this to go off.'

Father Michael's hand slowly emerged from his pocket and as it did so Mr Murphy could see a gold chain. More gold chains appeared until the eighteen carat gold filigree cross with a cultured pearl in the centre swung from Father Michael's hand catching the light. The pearl glowed.

It was impossible. Mr Murphy's hand left the trigger of the gun and trembling, he slowly reached out for the cross, taking it from Father Michael's hand. His mind went back to the time when his Grandma had opened his own small hand when they were alone in her bedroom and put the cross into it. He studied it closely. Yes. There was no doubt this it was his cross. He slowly looked up at Father Michael.

'Where...?' he said, his voice filled with emotion.

'I can't tell you about the man that came to my church to confess his sins and handed me the cross as it would be against my priestly vows to divulge anything said to me in confession. What I can say is that I have had this cross for many years and for some strange reason decided to bring it with me when we left Ireland. I have no idea why. I had the strongest feeling that it might belong to you. It clearly does and now it is back where it belongs.'

Flo moved around Father Michael and slowly extended her hand, taking the cross from Mr Murphy who made no effort to resist her. She walked around to the back of his chair and undid the clasp of the chain. She reached around his neck and put the cross on him. She spoke softly. Her voice had a sing-song quality to it almost as if a bird was calling her mate. Sean seemed to see a path of light in front of his eyes and a feeling of well being flooded through him smothering the hate and anger that had previously boiled up inside.

Father Michael was also experiencing a dream-like quality as he heard Flo's voice at the back of his mind calming and soothing him too. Time stood still for all of them except Flo. Her hands came up and her fingers rested lightly on Mr Murphy's temples.

'Your head is hurting and the pain has been awful. The pain has made you do bad deeds. You haven't been able to think clearly. You have been lost in the darkness. This cross is a symbol of the light and you are returning to the light.'

He heard her voice as if she was speaking to him from afar. He saw a carpet of bright flowers spilling joyously down a hill in a riot of colour: reds; yellow; blues and greens. The air he breathed seemed clear and fresh and the sky above him was blue. He saw a brilliant butterfly with gossamer wings hovering near him. Warmth flooded through his head as Flo gently massaged his temples. He saw silver and gold patterns whirling and swirling before his eyes and he laughed with the joy of it.

Distantly, he heard Flo saying, 'The pain will stop. The pain will stop. The pain will stop. Your headaches will go away.'

He slowly stood up, turning around to look at Flo and she seemed to shimmer. He brought his hands cautiously up to his head and held them there. His palms were sweating as he did so. He expected the searing pain to return any minute. But nothing happened. Nothing happened. He touched his cross. A slow smile passed across his face and he looked at Flo as if seeing her for the first time. He slowly turned to look at Sean and Father Michael who seemed mesmerised and were standing as if frozen in time.

Flo walked out from behind him and came in front of Father Michael and Sean. She turned to face him.

'Now it's gone,' said Flo looking at Mr Murphy with some affection, 'so perhaps you should take a little walk and I would be happy to come with you, if you wouldn't mind. We could take Anna for a walk with us.'

Sean and Father Michael couldn't believe their ears. They were astonished at the change in Mr Murphy. Indeed, his whole body seemed to be straighter and years had fallen from his face. Father Michael thought to himself that they had just witnessed a miracle. That God had worked his will through the cross and the little girl. Sean was confused and could hardly recall what had happened in the office but he knew that something profound had occurred and that Flo had been at the centre of it. Flo felt some energy slowly leaving her but still glowed from a spark deep inside. She knew for certain that Mr Murphy would let Anna go. She just knew it. He walked around to the front of his desk. Flo put her little hand trustingly into his and walked him gently towards the office door.

'We'll release Anna now and she can go home. Home to have her puppies with her family. You know where her home is don't you?' she said to Mr Murphy cocking her head to one side expecting his answer.

'Yes, I do. I have the address in my files.' he said distantly and he turned away from Flo, letting go of her hand and returning to his desk to open up the draw which held his files. He rummaged for a few moments and seemed to suddenly come out of a trance.

'Here. I have it. Anna's owner lives at this address in Plumstead. It's not far from here. We'll take my big Land Rover and drive there. What a Christmas present it will be for the family to have her back.'

Sean looked at Mr Murphy. He still couldn't get over the sudden transformation and now was suspicious of it. Father Michael was also confused at the sudden change even though he felt that the hand of God was present. Only Flo seemed completely at ease with his change of personality and treated him as if he was a kindly uncle.

'Come on, come on,' he said, walking towards the door with the file under his arm, 'there's no time to lose. Let's go. Wait, we still might need the gun.'

'No guns,' said Flo firmly. 'No need for guns anymore.'

'Well now Flo, I do feel different but there is still part of the old me bubbling inside.'

'And there always will be,' said Flo, 'but your job is to control that darkness and whenever you feel it coming back, touch your cross and remember the joy that you felt today.

He flung the door open and the others followed him, clattering down the iron staircase. Sean and Father Michael still wondered if it was all a trick and that he was only pretending to help them. The change in him seemed so unbelievable. Suddenly he stopped abruptly and they almost bumped into him. Flo flung up her hands to her head:

'No, No, not again,' cried Flo, 'Anna's gone. Burt has her. I know it. He means to harm her. Noooh.'

Tears ran down her cheeks and all her previous composure collapsed as she felt that her world was plunged into darkness.

Sean punched his big fist into his open hand and said to Mr Murphy, 'Did you know about this? Are you playing games with us?'

He looked genuinely shocked. 'No games Sean. I'm not sure what happened just now but I know that I feel different. It is hard to describe but it feels like a huge weight has just been lifted from me and now I mean to get Anna back. Not for me, but for Flo,' he said, squinting at the empty cage.

'Where would Burt take her?'

'To one of the kennels about five miles from here. He used to take the dogs there and shoot them if they were no good. I bet he's gone there. We must hurry or it may be too late.'

They ran towards the Land Rover and jumped in. Mr Murphy started the engine and the wheels spun as he wrenched the steering wheel around making the vehicle turn in a tight circle and splattering mud and water from the tyres. He gunned the engine for speed as they roared through the gates. No-one spoke. Why had Burt taken her? What was he going to do with her?   They feared the worst.

When Anna heard Burt's boots clattering down the iron staircase, she could smell the rage and anger that reeked from every pore in his body. She saw him moving towards her with Joe trailing close behind him. They were heading straight for the cage.

'Get the van over here.'

'Why do you want it?'

'Just get it here and do it now before I give you a smack.'

'Alright, alright but what are you gonna do?'

'Do? We've just been kicked out. No money, nothing. Nobody treats me like that. We're taking the dog and her puppies. We can sell the puppies and then get rid of the dog.'

'But Anna hasn't had the puppies yet and they might not be due for a few days.'

'Those puppies are ready to come out and I can get them out of her. Then I'll kill her.'

Joe recoiled when he heard Burt's words. He was horrified. He knew that Burt could be a bad man but he had never thought that he could be so cruel. He knew that Burt had put his rifle in the back of the van just that morning and so he must have been planning something like this anyway. But what could he do? If he tried to stop Burt, he would get hurt and Burt had beaten him once before, hitting and kicking him so hard that he had lost his front teeth. He was scared of

Burt. He thought that perhaps, once they were down at the kennels, then he could persuade him not to act so rashly, as Anna was still Mr Murphy's property. Yes, that was the way to play it. Burt would have to calm down and he would see sense. There was plenty of other work to be had in the security guard dog business. He would make Burt see this. Once Burt calmed down he would be bound to be scared of what Mr Murphy might do to him.

He felt more confident now. He would work on him as they were driving and Burt would come around to his way of thinking. After all, nobody wanted Mr Murphy's revenge. Yes. Once Burt had calmed down then he would see that.

Joe drove the van around, stopping in front of Anna's cage. Burt was in the shed putting some of his possessions into an old kitbag. Joe got out of the van holding the lead that he would attach to the chain around her neck. Anna trembled with fear and her puppies moved restlessly inside of her. She sensed that something bad was going to happen. She cowered and panted. Her heart thumped as Joe got nearer to the cage until he was standing in front of it. She looked up at him, turning her head to one side as she did so. She saw tears in Joe's eyes and smelt his fear too. He unlocked the cage door. He whispered Anna's name.

'Anna, Anna. I won't let him hurt you Anna.'

He bent down to attach the lead to the chain around Anna's neck and she could see every feature of his face which was so close to her that she could have bitten it in an instant. But she didn't. She waited. Suddenly Joe unclipped the black collar and pulled the chain back over her head.

'Go Anna,' he whispered, 'go, and get out of here.'

Anna heard the urgency in his voice and saw him step to one side of her cage. A knife flashed in his hand and for one second she thought that he would bring

the knife down on to her but he slashed his other hand
and blood dripped from his fingers.

'Help, help,' he shouted, 'the bleedin' dog just bit
me.'

The cage door was open. In one bound Anna was out
of the cage and running past the shed through the
yard gates and into the road. Her head turned to the
left as she sniffed the air and scented an invisible
pathway that she knew was there. One way or another,
she was going home.

Home. Freedom. No black box. Her family. So many
thoughts buzzed through Anna's mind as she ran out
of the gate and turned towards the pathway that
would take her home. She couldn't really run fast as
she lacked strength after the long ride back from
Ireland and also felt her puppies moving awkwardly
inside of her. Instinctively she knew that her time was
near and that the puppies would be born soon. She felt
an urgent need to return home to be with her owner
and the children. She tried to increase her pace.

There were many cars driving past in the road
beside her as she ran slowly on the pavement alongside
the canals. People were walking on the pavement.
When they saw Anna they stood aside as if they were
frightened but she didn't want to hurt anybody. She
ran towards the river following the pathway that led to
home but that scent became confusing.

She could feel the wind blowing towards her and the
wind brought other scents that were oily, damp, salty
and smoky. She smelt water and realised that her
destination lay on the other side of the river. She would
have to try to swim across no matter how dangerous it
would be for her and her puppies. She believed that she
could pick up the strong scent of home when she got
to the other side. Anna panted as she slowed down to
a walking pace in order to conserve her energy for the
swim ahead. She reached the edge of the bank of the

river and stopped to look down at it.

The river was wide. Very wide. It would be cold and Anna thought that her puppies wouldn't like that. Worse, she had had little to eat or drink since she had escaped and her energy levels were low. She could sense that Flo was still trying to reach out to her and she focused her mind on an image of Flo with her hair band with that little flower on the side that sought to keep those red curls away from her face. She tried her best to link to Flo but she was just too tired and the fear of the journey ahead disrupted her thoughts. She knew that she could drown in that river. Flo's image began to fade.

Anna saw some steps leading down towards the river and started to walk slowly towards them. She stopped and watched people walking towards a building with a dome on the top of it. They disappeared into the building at the same time as other people emerged. Where could they be going?

A pool of water lay by a rubbish bin next to the building and she slowly walked over to the pool, lapped at the water, grateful to be able to drink again even though the water tasted bad. Some bread had fallen out of the bin and was on the floor. She smelt meat inside the bread, found it and hastily gobbled up the remains of a burger. She needed all the strength that she could find.

Suddenly a big shadow loomed over her. Anna slowly turned her head. Burt. Burt reached out to grab her and in his hand he held a rope. He tried to put the rope over her head. She gave a low growl and gnashed her teeth to warn him off. He jumped back. She knew that she had to get away quickly and thought that instead of running towards the river that she could hide in the dome building. She ran away as quickly as she could and entered the open doorway. To her amazement she found herself looking at stairs that descended in a spiral pattern. She turned her head and saw Burt running towards her, shouting something. He was still holding the rope in his hands.

There was nothing else for it. She couldn't run back towards him and so she ran down the spiral staircase, although ran is the wrong word. She slipped, slid and fell painfully down the stairs banging her body against the hard wall. The stairs seemed endless. Down and down and down and down she went descending into a pit of dread. Fear coursed through her every fibre. Where was she running to? Anna had never felt so frightened in her life. She knew that Burt was the predator and if he caught her, she would be as good as dead.

She could hear the noise of machinery right next to the staircase but she had no time to worry about that as she could also hear Burt's boots clattering on the steps behind her. She had to get away but where was she running to? Finally the steps gave way to a flat surface and Anna could see a circular tunnel stretching out in front of her. Light reflected off the thousands of white tiles that lined the tunnel. She could smell the river and to her astonishment, the smell came from above. She could also smell fresh air coming from the tunnel exit in front of her. Now she knew her escape route.

People were walking towards her through the tunnel, including children. Perhaps the tunnel was safe after all. She started to run at a slow pace panting as she did so. She saw that quite a few people were pushing themselves to the side of the tunnel and holding their children close to them. She heard a commotion behind her. Burt was shouting. Whatever he was saying had the effect that now some people were trying to block her escape and catch her. She managed to avoid hands that were reaching for her and had to growl and bare her teeth at some of the would-be catchers in order to make them back off. But the smell of the fresh air entering the tunnel was stronger and the exit was getting nearer. She guessed that if she was under the water that she would have to climb a new set of stairs if she was to get to safety. Her energy was fading. How long could she keep running before Burt caught up with her? She had to escape but by now, Anna was barely able to run and could just about manage a fast walk. Her breathing became ragged and it was hard to think. Once again fear surged through her, releasing adrenaline and she pushed herself forward but she could hear Burt's boot clattering close behind and knew that he was gaining on her.

Suddenly a man jumped out in front of her and she had to swerve to avoid hitting him. Her tired body hit the side of the tunnel with a thump and her legs collapsed as she fell onto her side, panting hard.

Burt ran up and stood over her, his belly heaving from exertion. The rope collar dangled in his hand.

'Gotcha,' he said triumphantly.

Chapter Nine

Flo couldn't think clearly. She sat in the Land Rover next to Father Michael as Mr Murphy screamed down the road and tried rid her mind of confusion. She kept on getting flashes of reds, blues and yellows - vivid colours that made no sense to her although she could remember that Shelta had once described their meaning. Flo just could not think straight.

She decided to try to concentrate on her breathing and relax in order to calm her mind. She breathed the way Shelta had taught her which was very different from the shallow breathing that most people did. Shelta had told her to breathe just like a baby does. Control your breathing and you control your mind she said. Deep breaths: she let her tummy expand as she breathed in, and relax as she breathed out. She felt her mind slowly clearing. As her mind emptied of what Shelta called, 'monkey chatter,' she started to feel the emotions that Anna was experiencing as she approached the river and an image of water jumped into he head.

'Stop the car,' Flo shouted, 'Anna has escaped from Burt. She isn't going to the kennels; she's heading for the river. Stop the car.'

Mr Murphy screeched to a halt. 'Are you sure?' he said. 'Think carefully. Are you sure Flo?'

'Yes yes, I know that it's true. Anna has escaped but how can she cross the river if she is heading for home? She will drown.'

Mr Murphy gripped the steering wheel as he thought out loud. 'Anna can't swim across the river but if she is aiming for home she has to be making for

Greenwich. If she is going to Greenwich then she must use the tunnel under the river. There is no other way to cross the river and she must be thinking of getting home the fastest way.'

Flo looked at him. She then looked at her Da and Father Michael who nodded. Her eyes flicked back to Mr Murphy.

'We must go to Greenwich but then what do we do?'

Mr Murphy looked closely at her. His mind was clear and he hadn't felt like that for a very long time.

'We drive to Greenwich tunnel on the south side of the river. She has to come through the tunnel. We will meet her there. It's not far. Quickly now, let's go.'

With that he launched the Land Rover forward accelerating and narrowly missing an oncoming car on the corner.

'Watch out Murphy,' shouted Father Michael, 'or you'll kill us all and what good would that do Anna? Jaysus I don't want to meet God this quick!'

Father Michael gritted his teeth and felt sick. He was never good in cars at the best of times and now the Land Rover was lurching around corners at breakneck speed. In no time at all they had reached Greenwich and miraculously found a parking space, just by the Cutty Sark: a clipper ship in dry dock next to the tunnel. The doors of the Land Rover slammed shut as the group ran towards the tunnel entrance.

'No time to wait for the lift,' yelled Mr Murphy, 'we take the stairs. Flo, can you sense if Anna is near?'

'She is, she is,' said Flo breathlessly.

With Sean bringing up the rear and Father Michael still feeling sick from the motion of the car, they slowly ran down the stairs, passing surprised tourists who were ascending. But Flo and Mr Murphy bounded down the spiral staircase easily outstripping the rest of the group. Her little backpack, which she always had with her, bounced about on her back. She sometimes felt a sharp pinch in her spine but she thought nothing of it. Finally they reached the bottom of the stairwell having run down one hundred steps. They could hear the others trying their best to catch up. But where was Anna? There was no sign of her. Flo scrunched up her face in frustration.

'I was sure that she would be here.' Her hand strayed up to the amulet around her neck and it felt warm in her small hands. On impulse she shouted, 'Anna, Anna, Anna!'

Just as Burt was dragging Anna back along the tunnel Anna heard Flo's voice loud and clear in her mind. Suddenly energy seemed to flood through her again and she spun around in the direction of the voice and barked as loudly as she could. Burt savagely yanked the rope around her neck forcing her to follow him even though she was still trying to look back down the tunnel. The rope tightened around her throat and cut off her barks.

'Shut up if you know what's good for you. Shut up.' His big fist came down across Anna's snout making her yelp with pain and Burt pulled hard on the rope again but Anna knew that Flo was coming for her and that she was coming fast. Excitement flooded through her body and she put all her effort into not moving even though the pain in her neck was terrible as Burt tried to drag her back towards the tunnel entrance.

'Move it. Move it NOW,' Burt shouted.

He bent down to pick Anna up thinking that he could use the lift to get her out of the tunnel. Burt was so strong that there was nothing that Anna could do to stop him. With Anna in his arms Burt stumbled forward nearing the tunnel lift.

'Get out of my way. I have a sick dog that needs emergency help. Move aside! Keep that lift door open for me!'

Burt tried to increase his pace towards the lift as

Anna struggled in his arms. She was crushed to his chest. She tried in vain to bite him but her head was just out of reach of his body. She felt her puppies moving awkwardly inside her as Burt's enormous arms exerted more and more pressure on her chest. Hope began to fade away.

The rescuers ran down the tunnel, scattering the pedestrians who flattened themselves to its sides.

'I can see Burt,' shouted Flo. 'He has Anna in his arms. Quick! They are not far ahead of us.'

The group, with Sean panting and wheezing in the rear, increased their pace just as Burt, who was nearing the lift, had to stop in order to prevent Anna from falling out of his arms. He was panting and wheezing with the effort of running and sweat ran down the sides of his quivering jowls splashing on his grimy shirt. He was almost at the lift when Mr Murphy sprinted past him, stopped and turned quickly pointing a finger straight towards his eyes.

'Put her down Burt,' he commanded, 'put her down and walk away. She belongs to me.' Burt lowered Anna to the tunnel floor. 'She's mine by right. You fired me. Remember? No wages. The dog is mine and you can't do anything about it. I worked for you and you treated me like dirt. Well that's over now. Do your worst but the dog is mine.'

Mr Murphy was just about to take a step forward when Sean suddenly appeared behind Burt like an unstoppable runaway truck. Sean threw himself forward and grabbed Burt around the knees. The two huge men clashed and hit the floor but Burt quickly turned on to his back bringing his knee up into Sean's groin. Sean grimaced with pain and had to roll away from Burt who staggered up, finding his feet. Mr Murphy moved forward to stop him but Burt lowered his bulk and charged forward knocking him out the way as if he were made of paper. Sean started to run after him but Father Michael caught hold of him.

'Let him go. You can deal with him later if you must but we need to get Anna home quickly. By the look of her, those puppies will not be long in coming.'

Anna was lying down on the floor panting. Flo bent down to cuddle her and then, on impulse, she took off the amulet that was around her neck and tied it around Anna's neck. The metal felt warm to the touch and immediately Anna felt strength flowing through her. She felt strong again. She got to her feet, and barked excitedly wagging her tail. She barked again and started to walk down the tunnel turning her head around in order to look directly at Flo.

Flo's voice rang out with confidence. 'Anna wants us to go with her now. She wants to go home and seems much stronger.'

Mr Murphy looked at this young girl who seemed so fragile but had iron running through her veins. He looked at Father Michael who nodded.

'Right, let's get Anna to the Land Rover and take her home.'

Mr Murphy looked back down the tunnel and saw that Burt was still standing near the lift. Burt shook his fist in the air and then, with his voice echoing all through the tunnel shouted, 'This ain't over, you hear me? This ain't over by a long shot.'

The door to the lift opened and Burt stepped into it and disappeared from sight.

The flow of energy that Anna had experienced was ebbing away although she still felt a warm tingle running through her body and she slowed her pace down to a walk. She was clearly exhausted by the events. Mr Murphy ran up beside her and crouched down. He stroked her head and whispered soothing words into her ear. By this time Flo, Father Michael and Sean had caught up although Sean was moving slowly, clearly in some pain.

'Anna can't walk much further.' Mr Murphy looked very concerned. 'We will have to carry her but she is heavy.'

Sean walked forward and carefully bent down. He looked into Anna's eyes and Anna licked his hand. Flo was beside him.

'Da, can you carry her up the stairs?' she said, 'as I think that she really needs our help now.'

'Wait a minute,' said Father Michael excitedly, 'there's a lift that we can use to get to the top. If Sean can carry her to the lift then we can get her to the car which is close by. Can you carry her Sean? I know that Burt hurt you.'

'Not a bother,' said Sean and he slowly bent down, putting his arms gently around Anna. With a grunt, he lifted Anna high in the air holding her tenderly in front of his body. Flo could feel her Da's heart racing with the effort that he was making but knew that he was determined to do what was needed.

'C'mon, let's move,' said Sean and he staggered forward towards the tunnel exit.

'I'll run ahead and get the lift down for us and make sure that no one else can use it,' said Father Michael.

The group moved down the tunnel and Anna felt safe in Sean's huge arms with Flo walking beside her. Her puppies stirred, pushing against each other and she knew that soon nature would take its course. Father Michael held the lift doors open, standing at the front and preventing anyone else getting in. He kept saying to anyone who asked why they couldn't enter.

'Sorry, I'm on a mission. This is God's work.'

A small crowd had now gathered by the lift and they were becoming agitated as Father Michael held the doors open but the rescuers arrived behind them and the sight of Sean holding Anna with Mr Murphy and

Flo by his side, caused a gap as reluctantly the crowd parted. Flo suddenly stopped just before she entered the lift and turned towards the small crowd.

'Thank you for waiting. This is my dog Anna and she is about to have puppies. She has had a terrible time and has been abused. This is an emergency. We need to get her to safety and that is why we need to use the lift. Thank you for your understanding.'

The small crowd heard her words in silence and then slowly, one by one, began to clap until everybody was clapping and cheering. Cries of 'Good luck Anna,' rang around the tunnel and the crowd cheered as the lift doors closed and the group began to ascend to the top. The rescuers could still hear the crowd's good will echoing up the lift shaft as the doors opened into bright daylight.

The Land Rover wasn't far and soon the group all were inside. Anna lay in the back snuggled between Father Michael and Flo who was stroking and sending her soothing thoughts.

The engine started and the Land Rover moved off. Anna closed her eyes and rested, feeling the puppies move inside her but she knew that she was going home at last. Her hope was that the puppies would be born in her old home with her owner, the children, Flo and her new friends.

Mr Murphy drove towards Woolwich and Anna's home in Plumstead. There were Christmas lights along the route in all the shops. Some adults and children were wearing red Santa Claus hats and there was a feeling of excitement in the air as the younger children thought about the presents that Father Christmas would bring them. Shops were playing Christmas carols and happy jingles and shoppers showed good will towards each other. Flo hadn't even thought about Christmas until she had looked out of the window. She sometimes wound the window down to hear the festive music. She suddenly thought that she hadn't even bought her Da a card or a present but perhaps getting Anna back safe and sound to her home would be present enough for everyone.

Flo automatically shifted her backpack to one side as once again she felt a pricking in her back but she thought nothing of it. She settled down in her seat absently stroking Anna. For the first time in ages, Flo felt that all was well.

At that moment, the car crashed into them.

Burt wasn't just angry, he was absolutely furious. As soon as he had pushed Sean away he had turned towards the tunnel entrance to make his escape. He broke into a slow trot. He couldn't run fast as his enormous bulk normally prevented that sort of movement, but once he was on the move nothing could stop him. He was like a runaway lorry.

His face was twisted into a scowl, and all in front of him moved quickly out of his way. They flattened themselves against the sides of the tunnel in order to avoid being mown down as he ponderously made his way towards the tunnel entrance. He saw the lift doors closing and shouted but it was too late, the lift was gone. He thought that Mr Murphy would come after him and this spurred him into action.

He would have to force himself to climb one hundred stairs in order to escape from the tunnel but Burt's rage spurred him on and he pushed himself as fast as he could, attacking the stairs and sweating profusely as he did so. Finally he reached the top and burst out into a day which was now bright with a blue sky. He shielded his eyes against the glare of the sun sinking slowly down on the horizon and the water in the river Thames sparkled as the sunlight danced upon the waves.

A charity man dressed in a Santa Claus outfit and

holding a collection box was thinking of approaching Burt to ask for a donation but on seeing his face he shrank back. Burt knew exactly what he was going to do. He knew that Anna would be heading for her previous owner's address and he knew exactly where that was. He had his gun in the back of the van. This was the same gun that he used to put down dogs that didn't meet his standards. His standards were that a dog had to be ferocious and ready to attack. There was no point in keeping a dog if the dog was useless as a guard dog. Burt had used his gun many times. He now intended to use his gun on Anna.

He had a plan. He would drive to Plumstead where he would lie in wait. Sooner or later he knew that Anna would appear and when that happened he would be ready. He was sure that nobody would expect him to take his revenge in this manner. Burt was past caring about what Mr Murphy could do to him. Yes, he was afraid of the man, but now he just didn't care. As far as he was concerned, he was at war. Yes, war.

His anger fuelled itself. The more he thought about the way Murphy had treated him, the angrier he became. Burt had murder on his mind and a red mist descended blocking out every other thought, except revenge. He couldn't risk shooting Murphy, but he would shoot his dog. He turned the key in the ignition of the van and the engine roared into life. He smiled to himself. Nothing would prevent him from taking his revenge.

He arrived at Churchill Road in Plumstead and parked the van up the street away from Anna's house. To his surprise there was no sign of Anna or the others. Good, he thought. They must have been delayed. Time for me to set up.

He looked for a suitable place to park the van. It had to be close enough to Anna's house for a clear shot but in a good spot for a quick getaway. He needed the van to be partly hidden, as he intended to rest his gun on the top of the roof, disguising the barrel by putting an old hessian bag over it. To a passerby it should look like he was just leaning on the van but he suspected that when Anna arrived home and was greeted by her owner and the children, all eyes would be on her and no one would spot him.

Homecoming. Burt snorted and squeezed his eyes shut slowly opening them. His eyes felt sore and gritty. He shook his head. Homecoming. He would spoil their party. Nothing like a dead dog to do that and serve them right for treating him so badly. He looked up and down the street. It was quiet and getting dark. He could see Christmas lights lighting up the windows of many of the houses as they twinkled. Warm colours of reds, yellows and blues flashed on and off, sending messages of goodwill.

Christmas. He hated Christmas. He recalled his drunken dad staggering into their tiny house late on Christmas eve and the shouting that went on between his Mum and Dad. Burt snorted. His Dad hadn't even spelt his name correctly on his birth certificate as he was probably drunk. His name should have been spelled 'Bert' not 'Burt'. Christmas eve.

He remembered being in his tiny bedroom, huddled under the bedclothes trying to block out the bad sounds that he heard. The inevitable noise of the outside door slamming made tears spring to his eyes and he trembled as he listened to the sound of his mum sobbing.

He hated Christmas. Nothing but bad memories.

He shook his head as if trying to rid himself of the past and once again looked up and down the street, searching for the right place. There it was. Just behind the telegraph pole on the corner of the street that led into Churchill Road. A car was parked near the corner. If he parked behind it, then the van would be hidden from view. Additionally he would also be partially obscured as the telegraph pole would shield him. Yes, the perfect place.

He started up the van and moved it behind the car and next to the telegraph pole. Still there was no one about. All was quiet although the faint sound of Christmas carols floated through the air.

Carols. He hated carols. Always singing about how happy everyone was because Jesus was born. What a load of rubbish. There was no God. If there was, why had God let his Dad hurt his Mum? Why had his drunken dad taken a belt to him when he had done nothing wrong? Why had the dog bitten him all those years ago when all he was doing was playing? No, the only God that Burt respected was the fist and the boot. Fear was what made the world go round.

Burt hated to be ignored. He would push people's buttons in order to provoke a reaction and then he would keep pushing. He was certain that killing Anna was justified. In his mind he had been wronged. He hated rejection and Murphy had done just that by kicking him out without giving him a penny. Murphy had ridiculed and embarrassed him in front of Joe, who was a low life in Burt's mind.

There was no alternative. Burt didn't think about the consequences of what he was going to do. He would deal with them later and he didn't mind going to prison anyway. He had been there before and had used his brute strength to get what he wanted. No, the thought of prison didn't bother him and who would mind about a dead dog anyway? He got back into the van and lit a cigarette. He patted the gun now wrapped in a hessian covering which disguised its deadly appearance.

He was concerned about the light. Darkness was falling and that might interfere with his aim but once the front door of the house opened there would be plenty of light and he just had to wait for the right

time to shoot. He was confident that he could hit
Anna. He was a good shot. His spell in the army, when
he ran away from home, had at least taught him how
to shoot straight. He hated the army too. Smoke slowly
rose from the cigarette in his hand making ghostly
shapes. He settled down to wait.

Crash! The world went crazy for the rescuers as the
vehicle spun around in a circle thrown by the force of
the collision. Anna hit the back of the Land Rover's
seats and lay stunned on the floor under a tangle
of feet. Flo and Father Michael had also hit the seats
in front of them but had protected themselves by
throwing their arms in front of their faces. They
seemed to be dazed but otherwise unharmed.

Sean in the passenger seat had hit his head on the
dashboard and some blood was oozing down the side of
his head from a cut. Mr Murphy had been thrown
towards the windscreen and had also banged his head
and was stunned but unhurt. He was however very
angry and flung open his door aiming to confront the
careless driver of the car that hit them.

A small elderly man stood shaking by the side of his
little grey car. The car's bonnet was creased and a
headlight dangled down. Steam and smoke were
coming out from underneath the bonnet. He trembled
from head to foot.

'I'm sorry I'm so... so... sorry,' he stammered. 'I just
didn't see you. I was going to get the ferry and was in
a hu... hu... hurry. Oh dear, oh dear.' He wrung his
hands and his head bobbed from side to side in
agitation.

Mr Murphy looked at him as if he could tear his
head off but seeing how old and shaken the man was
his anger left him.

'Are you right ? Jaysus you nearly killed us all. It's
lucky that my car is solid or you would have turned us

over. Jaysus' mother have mercy. What a mess.'

The Land Rover was stuck at a very busy round-about and now the traffic had stopped and people were getting out of their cars to see what had happened. Many offered help and soon the sound could be heard of sirens as an ambulance and possibly a police car approached.

Mr Murphy ran around and opened the rear door. He shot out a barrage of questions.

'How you doing? How's Anna? Sean you're bleeding. Listen to me. The cops will turn up soon and they will tie us up for ages. Does anyone need to go to hospital? Are Anna's pups OK?'

Flo and Father Michael had lifted Anna back up onto the rear seat. She seemed dazed and confused. Flo looked at Anna and reached out to her asking her if she was hurt. Anna licked her hand in answer and moved her body in response although she couldn't stand up properly.

'Sean, how are you?' Father Michael asked. He was concerned to see blood trickling down his face.

'I'm fine. Just a scratch but that doesn't bother me. How are we going to get Anna home now? We've no transport and by the look of her, her time is due. Let's get out of this car and get onto the pavement away from harm.'

Sean opened the rear door to the Land Rover and carefully lifted Anna into his arms. He walked across the road and stepped on to the pavement, closely followed by Father Michael and Flo. Mr Murphy was at their heels.

'Look. A bus is coming and that bus will take you to Plumstead garage. Churchill Road is just around the corner and that's where Anna came from. The bus will only take about fifteen minutes and she can be home. If we wait here and try to sort out another car it will take time which we can't afford. Get the bus. I'll stay and sort out this mess. Now go and good luck. I'll try to catch you up later'

'What about the police?' asked Sean.

'Not a bother. Leave them to me. Now go.'

There it was. A big red double decker bus with the open entrance at the back. The bus would stop at the bus stop which was only yards away from where the rescuers were standing. Father Michael took charge.

'Right Sean, you carry Anna onto the bus. Flo, don't forget your backpack which is on the back seat of the car. You had better get it. Quickly now.'

Flo turned and ran across the road, opened the car door and grabbed her backpack. Just having the backpack in her hands seemed to fill her with confidence that all would be well and she quickly returned to the bus stop, smiling as she did so.

They looked like a strange group. Sean still had blood trickling down one side of his face despite trying to mop it up with his handkerchief; Flo had her backpack in her hands and looked like she had been dragged through a hedge backwards; Father Michael's jacket was torn, one sleeve flapped about and his dog collar now had blood splattered on it, perhaps from the cut on Sean's face. Anna was exhausted but was content for Sean to carry her.

The bus conductor's face dropped when he saw the rescuers about to board his bus. He was a small man, neatly dressed in his conductor's uniform with his ticket machine dangling around his neck. This was his bus and he decided who would ride in it. There was no way that this ragbag of humanity, with a huge dog that looked half dead, was boarding his bus.

He pulled himself up to his full height and thrust out his arm spreading his fingers. His voice rang with the authority of one who is used to getting his way.

'Stop right there. You are not getting on my bus. Now, hop it.'

Sean very slowly and carefully put Anna down onto the pavement. He straightened up and put one foot on the platform of the bus grabbing hold of the pole which ran from floor to ceiling. The bus actually tipped as he swung himself up and into the bus, pushing the conductor backwards with his big belly.

He spoke slowly in a deep voice. 'Now listen to me. This dog is about to have pups. We have just been bashed about in a car crash. I have hit my head on the front of the car. I have had my nadgers kicked by a madman in a fight as he was trying to steal the dog. My daughter has been chased all over Ireland by kidnappers and we have a priest with us who is doing his best to help us get the dog back to her owner before the pups are born. Now all we need is a ride to Plumstead bus garage. Surely that's not too much to ask, is it?'

The passengers who were sitting inside the bus had listened to Sean's confusing tale but there was no doubt where their sympathies lay.

'Let them on the bus. Let them on the bus. Let them on the bus,' they shouted and one fierce looking woman with frizzy blond hair ran down the aisle and grabbed the conductor by his arm.

'You bleedin' let them on the bus you officious git, or I'll throw you off the bus myself.'

On hearing this, the passengers both inside and those waiting to board at the bus stop cheered.

Sean turned around, stepped off the bus and picked Anna up again and one by one the rescuers boarded the bus. The passengers downstairs stood and gave their seats up, clapping and cheering as the bus set off. Father Michael went back to the conductor and paid for their fares. The conductor didn't say one word as he issued the tickets.

Anna knew that she was on her way home again. She felt so weary that she could hardly think but she knew that she had to keep her strength up as she would need it to birth her puppies and there would be many to birth.

At the front of the bus, a ruddy-faced large man, who might have taken a drink or two, stood up. He was wearing a Santa hat which was too small for his head. He turned towards all the other passengers and started to sing.

'We wish you a merry Christmas. We wish you a merry Christmas....'

Everyone joined in and there was laughter, singing and good cheer as the passengers asked the rescuers what had happened and listened in astonishment when Flo and Father Michael recounted part of their adventures. Anna felt sure that her owner and family were still living at the house. Her home was now only minutes away and she felt the amulet around her neck becoming warmer. Her body started to feel as if it was waking up and energy was beginning to flow through her again. Flo felt the change too.

Anna was really going home, at last.

Chapter 10

When the bus arrived at the terminus, Sean stepped down from the platform and put Anna onto the ground. Anna sniffed the air. The path to her house was so clear to her that she could almost see it. Anna wagged her tail and barked excitedly.

Flo, Sean, and Father Michael stood looking at Anna as she slowly started to move out of the bus terminus. Flo could hear a babble of voices behind her as she walked forward.

'Where are they going?'

'The dog is going home and it's only around the corner I think.'

'Why don't we go with her and see what happens when she gets home?'

'Good idea. What about a Christmas carol as we walk behind her?'

'I'll sing one,' said the man in the jolly Santa hat and in a lovely voice he started to sing the carol called *Good King Wenceslas* which had a happy sound to it.

'I'll join you.' The bus conductor smiled nervously as Sean turned around to look at him but then broke into a smile.

'Of course you will. Youse are all welcome to come with us,' said Sean putting his huge arm around the bus conductor's shoulders and they set off together with Sean in great voice bellowing out the carol. Flo felt a slight prick in her back and remembered that she had that old stick of wood in her rucksack. She thought that it would make a very good baton to lead the crowd singing. She reached into her bag and pulled it out from the bottom. The oak stick felt warm in her hands and she walked backwards for a few steps waving her arms around as if conducting an orchestra before turning and following Anna while still conducting the singers.

As the noisy crowd turned into Churchill Road, doors began to open as householders heard the carol singing. When they asked what was happening they got an excited reply from the group and learned that Anna had been lost for a long time and was now returning home to number thirty six to have her pups. Many of the householders knew Anna's owner, May, who still lived at the house, and joined the party. Some even brought out mince pies to give to the group as they launched into another carol. There was much laughter and good cheer and spirits rose at the sound of it all.

Finally Anna crossed the road and sat down on the pavement in front of her old home. There was a small white Christmas tree in the window of the house which twinkled with coloured lights and a wreath with red ribbons hung on the door. The gate was shut. Father Michael walked forward and opened it. The festive group stayed on the other side of the road watching with great anticipation.

'Flo, you ring the doorbell,' said Father Michael, 'it should be you they see first as Anna wouldn't be here without your help. Go on now.'

Flo stepped forward in front of Anna who followed her through the gate. Anna sat on the small patch of green grass outside the front window looking at the door. Flo walked slowly up the path towards the door. She was nervous but she still had the oak stick in her left hand as she rang the doorbell. There was complete silence until she heard footsteps approaching the front door. The light above the door switched on and illuminated the path and the small garden. The door was opened cautiously and a small boy's face peered out through the gap looking at Flo. It was Alfie. He opened the door wider and Flo stepped to one side so that he could see Anna. Anna gave an excited bark and stood up wagging her tail.

'It's Anna, it's Anna, Anna,' cried Alfie, rushing out

of the door and flinging his arms around Anna's neck
hugging her tightly. 'Mum, Lizzie, Eve, come quickly,
it's Anna,' he shouted excitedly.

Lizzie was the first through the door followed by Eve.
They stopped and looked at Anna and then started
to cry rushing forward to join Alfie and hugging and
kissing Anna as she tried to lick their faces. The crowd
across the road began to cheer and clap and create a
great noise. Santa hat began to sing, 'We wish you a
Merry Christmas.'

Anna's owner, May, came to the door, looking at the
crowd in astonishment. Anna looked at her and held her
eyes. Alfie, Eve and Lizzie stood up.

'Anna, is it you? Can it be you? Oh Anna, Anna.'
May ran over to Anna and cuddled her while kneeling
on the grass. She kissed Anna's head and Anna licked
her face. May ran her hands down Anna's flanks.
'Anna, you have puppies. I can feel them. You are
almost due. Oh Anna, we have missed you so much.
Thank God that you are alive. How did you get here?
Where have you been? Oh Anna, we love you so much.'

Father Michael stepped forward.

'Hello, I am Father Michael and this little girl is
called Flo and her Dad, Sean rescued Anna and brought
her back. There is a lot of tale to be told but why don't
we get Anna into your house? You are right. Her
puppies will be born soon. I know that we are strangers
but perhaps we could come in to help you and tell you
all about her adventures.'

May stood up. Many of her neighbours over the road
called out to her and there was much laughter as
strangers hugged each other and clapped just from the
warmth and love that they could plainly see. Many
tears ran down a face that night. An unforgettable
night.

May said in a clear voice, 'Thank you all for bringing
Anna back to us. This has been one of the best days of

our lives. I don't know what else to say. Merry Christmas.'

The crowd clapped and shouted good wishes as May turned back towards the house and spoke to Father Michael, Flo and Sean.

'Please come in. We are not ready for guests so take us as you find us but you are all welcome here.'

Eve took Flo's hand and led her up the steps and into the house. Alfie and Lizzie followed.

Lizzie stopped, turned around and said,' Come on Anna, you're home now. We'll take care of you and never let you go again. You're safe now. Come on Anna.'

Father Michael and Sean stood behind Anna and started to walk towards the steps but Anna stopped suddenly as if she had run into a brick wall. That smell. The smell that she hated. It was near. Close. The smell of Burt hit Anna's senses so hard that she began to stagger. Anna recovered her balance and turned her head and body looking straight where she knew that Burt was concealed. Her body trembled and she began to growl and bare her teeth ready to spring forward in his direction. Just at the same time that Burt squeezed the trigger.

The bullet left the barrel travelling at over seven hundred metres per second. Nothing could stop it from killing Anna.

Flo's mind reeled from the intensity of Anna's hate for Burt. She spun around in his direction. As she did so her arm came up with lighting speed and pointed the oak stick at him. A blinding blue flash took place at the tip of the stick just as the bullet hit Anna with great force knocking her backwards. Anna sank to the ground. Flo shouted Burt's name and had already begun to run towards him, unaware that he had pulled the trigger. Sean also saw Burt and started to run towards the van. There was chaos as the family and the crowd surged around Anna not understanding what had happened. They saw Anna lying motionless on the grass.

May dropped to her knees crying, 'Anna, Anna.'

Burt knew that he had killed Anna. He had seen the bullet's impact dropping Anna to the ground. His aim between her eyes had been true. There was no doubt in his mind. Now he intended to jump into the van, start the engine and roar off around the corner before anyone knew what had happened. But he hadn't bargained with just how fast Sean could run. Sean was sprinting towards the van shouting at him with his fists clenched. Burt knew that there was no time to get into the van but thought that if he could run across the road to the alleyway then he could escape and hide in the dark until it all blew over. He didn't have time to think it all out but he knew that Sean was angry enough to really hurt him. Escape was all he thought about.

Dropping the gun and light on his feet with fear, Burt quickly turned away from the van and ran across the road towards the dark alleyway which ran parallel with the back of the terraced houses. He focused on nothing but the alleyway as he ran into the middle of the road. Suddenly he saw two headlights fast approaching.

The old Land Rover which was kept in the yard, now driven by Joe, smashed into him. Joe recognised Burt instantly. The Land Rover shuddered to a halt as Burt was thrown up into the air landing heavily on its bonnet with an enormous crash and then he was tossed up over the roof like a rag doll before finally coming to rest in a heap on the road behind it. The Land Rover screeched to a halt.

Why was Joe there? Joe's conscience had stricken him. He had known that Burt would try to kill Anna and he had decided to try to stop him. He had no plan but had felt compelled to drive to Anna's home. He was prepared to do anything he could to stop Burt hurting Anna even if he got himself hurt in the process. Joe had done a lot of bad things in his life but he had felt something for Anna the first time that he saw her and had flinched from Burt's cruelty towards her. The least that he could do was to let Anna go home safely to her family.

Joe's head hit the steering wheel as the Land Rover came to an abrupt stop. Somehow he wasn't the least bit surprised that he had hit Burt, even though he didn't mean to. Stunned, he got out of the Land Rover just as Sean and Flo arrived. Burt was lying in the road. He wasn't moving. Sean knelt down beside him and touched his neck feeling for his pulse.

'He's gone. He's gone.'

Joe stood in the road shaking. 'I didn't mean to hit him. Honest. He just ran out in front of me. I didn't mean it, honest.'

Sean put his arm across Joe's shoulders. 'It's nobody's fault Joe. We have to call the police. Cover him with a blanket. Come on, we'll do it at Anna's house.'

Flo turned around and started to run back towards the garden where Anna lay on the grass surrounded by her family. She burst through the group of onlookers. May was still cradling Anna's head in her hands, softly rocking her.

Flo shouted, 'Anna's not dead. She's not dead. I would have felt it. Anna's alive.' She crouched down and looked closely at Anna's neck. The amulet was bent and twisted as if hit by a great force. As she glanced downwards, a piece of dull metal, on glinting in the light on the grass, caught her eye. The bullet. The bullet had hit the amulet and not Anna. It had been deflected away from her head. The sheer force of the impact had knocked Anna out. Somehow a miracle had happened.

All Flo could remember was pointing the stick at Burt. Where was the stick now? It was gone. She let her mind flow towards Anna who felt her presence. Anna felt her senses coming back and slowly opened her eyes. She licked Flo's hand.

'She's alive,' May gasped as tears ran down her face. 'She's alive, she's alive.'

The crowd around Anna cheered and clapped. Some danced and threw their hats into the air. The jolly Santa man shouted, 'Happy Christmas. Happy Christmas.'

'Let's get her into the house,' said Father Michael. 'Sean, will you lift her?'

Sean bent down and carefully picked Anna up. He walked up the steps and into the house making for the kitchen. May told Lizzie to go into the shed and bring out Anna's old bed and blanket and Sean put Anna down carefully into her bed. The smells that Anna had once loved so much flooded her senses. Alfie held a bowl of water close to Anna and she lapped up the water, feeling more energy flowing back into her battered body. She struggled to push herself up and let out a whimper.

Anna's puppies were finally coming.

Anna had never given birth to puppies before but it was as nature intended. Animals instinctively know what to do. The pups inside her were wriggling and started to move down the birth canal ready to be born. May had already made a comfortable bed for Anna. She had more blankets and soft towels ready to hand to assist Anna as she gave birth. She banished everyone from the kitchen telling them that if she needed help then she would ask for it. Flo felt that she wanted to be with Anna but respected May's wishes knowing that she could still send her strength, warmth and love. Anna looked at May with her brown doleful eyes and trustingly licked May's hand. She whimpered and panted. May gently stroked her head.

'You can do this Anna and I will be here to help you and your puppies. I promise that I will never let you down again.'

Within minutes a puppy was born and covered in the special sac which protected each pup in the womb. Anna instinctively licked away the birth sac and to May's pure delight saw that the first pup was a honey coloured bitch, just like Anna.

All pups are born with their eyes closed and the first born made mewing noises just like a cat and moved around as if she was exploring her new world. Anna was so proud of herself, but still in some discomfort. She looked up at May.

'Well done Anna, but you have a few more pups to be born.'

Not long after the first pup, Anna whimpered again and sure enough another bitch pup was born. May started to become concerned as an hour had passed since she had given birth. Anna was clearly in pain but no pup was coming out. She became more and more distressed, looking at May for help. May could see that the next pup was struggling to be born. Instead of its head coming out first, there was a back leg showing and this would make the birth more difficult for Anna and might be dangerous for her.

May picked up one of the soft towels and held the back leg of the pup. She gently pulled forward the other leg which was stuck in the birth canal. It was a breech birth and May caressed the pup and pulled a little at a time until the pup started to emerge. This pup was so much bigger than the other two. It was a dog and he was black and tan. She helped rub off the sac as Anna was really exhausted from the birth.

May smiled as the newborn whimpered. She thought that the chubby little pup was so lovable that she named him Tubby.

Tubby made a louder mewing noise and found his way straight to Anna in order to suckle milk. Thankfully after the big puppy had been born the next five were born head first and caused no further problems for her. Altogether there were eight healthy puppies born. Four were bitches and four were dogs. What a mixture they were. Their fur was either honey coloured, brown or black and brown.

May wiped all the puppies with the soft towel and gave Anna a well deserved bowl of milk and raw eggs which were full of protein to give her energy after the exhausting birth of the puppies. It had taken Anna three hours to give birth but the puppies we all now suckling and bonding with her. Soon they snuggled down for sleep and Anna closed her big brown eyes and also fell asleep, happy and content as only a mother can be when she knows the miracle of birth.

May was exhausted by the events of the day. She looked down at Anna and saw that the first pup born looked just like her. May was determined that Flo, who had risked so much to bring Anna home, would have the first born and that she too would be named Anna. May opened the door quietly to the sitting room and eager, expectant eyes looked up at her. She gave them all the news about the puppies and said they could now come into the kitchen quietly as Anna was sleeping after her exhausting birthing. There was hardly enough space in the kitchen for everyone but they huddled up leaving room for Anna and the pups.

Tears flowed. Tears ran down their cheeks as they realised what a miracle they were seeing. They held hands and warmth and love flowed through them making a bond that could never be explained. Dawn finally came. The sun began to shine through the frosty panes. Outside it was cold and the snowflakes that had floated down during the night coated the garden in a

white blanket. It was still snowing. The rays of sun lit
up the room in an orange glow where all the family and
new friends were now quietly snoozing, except for May
who was still with Anna. It had been a long long night.
The lights on the Christmas tree twinkled on and off
throwing warm colours across the walls, lighting up
the gaily wrapped presents surrounding the tree. The
embers of the fire in the hearth glowed and Anna, now
partially awake, could hear the sound of crackling
flames weaving their way around the logs.

All was quiet and peaceful on Christmas morning.
Anna lay in her warm bed, exhausted by her labours.
Her puppies snuggled into her. She looked at May who
was sleeping quietly in the kitchen chair, put her head
on to her paws and stretched. Home.

Epilogue

Mr Murphy arrived at the house later on Christmas
day bringing with him food and drink. He was in great
spirits and told them all about what had happened after
the crash and how he had dealt with the police and
the ambulance. They had taken the old man who had
hit them to hospital as he was dazed and confused.
Mr Murphy had gone with him and stayed overnight
until his relatives were contacted and able to come and
see him on Christmas day. He had then left, and having
found a shop that was open, bought what he could, and
then taken a taxi to May's house.

The police arrived after Burt's death and took Joe to
the police station but let him go after a witness explained what had happened. The police were satisfied
that the accident was not Joe's fault. Joe made his way
back to May's house in order to apologise for the harm
that had been done to Anna, and May invited him in.
Joe was reluctant at first until Sean came out to him
and physically pulled him inside. He was frightened

when he saw that his boss, Mr Murphy, was there too but Mr Murphy greeted him warmly. Joe was delighted to see Anna safe and sound surrounded by her puppies and tears ran down his face as he stood beside her.

There was hardly any room in May's sitting room and lounge for them all but what there was, including food and drink, was shared in the spirit of a Christmas that none would forget.

Flo left the others and walked out of the kitchen, cuddling Anna and the unborn pups on the way to the garden. She was delighted that May had given her Anna's first born, who would be Flo's own Anna. Flo felt that she needed some personal time alone. So much had happened to her. She felt different somehow. She felt that she had grown up quickly and had left far behind the little girl that she once was.

She felt strong and her fingers tingled as if energy was sparking through them. She thought of Shelta and of all that Shelta had taught her. Flo knew that she had many talents but that she still had so much to learn. She wondered if she was a white witch: someone who had extraordinary powers but who could use them for the good of others. It didn't matter. She was so happy to have made new friends of Lizzie, Evie and Alfie and felt a real bond with them. They felt like family to her. She also felt that she had a bond for life with Father Michael, Mr Murphy and even Joe who had all played a part in bringing Anna safely home.

As the snow slowly settled on her red hair, she felt a soothing presence flood through her mind and images of brightly coloured butterflies in a field of spring flowers appeared before her eyes.

Her face slowly broke out into a beautiful smile and she threw her hands up into the air as she danced in the snow.